THE ISLAND
OF LAST TRUTH

Flavia Company

THE ISLAND
OF LAST TRUTH

*Translated from the Catalan
by Laura McGloughlin*

Europa
editions

Europa Editions
214 West 29th Street
New York, N.Y. 10001
www.europaeditions.com
info@europaeditions.com

Translation by Laura McGloughlin
Original title: *L'illa de l'última veritat*
Translation copyright © 2012 by Europa Editions
The translation of this work was supported
by a grant from the Institut Ramon Llull

LLLL institut
ramon llull
Catalan Language and Culture

Library of Congress Cataloging in Publication Data is available
ISBN 978-1-60945-081-6

Company, Flavia
The Island of Last Truth

Book design by Emanuele Ragnisco
www.mekkanografici.com

Prepress by Grafica Punto Print – Rome

Printed in the USA

Toast

Now I have an island, I wish to toast C.C.,
who is the sea in which it lies.

I have attempted here to lay bare with the unreserve of a last hour's confession the terms of my relation with the sea, which beginning mysteriously, like any great passion the inscrutable Gods send to mortals, went on unreasoning and invincible, surviving the test of disillusion, defying the disenchantment that lurks in every day of a strenuous life; went on full of love's delight and love's anguish, facing them in open-eyed exultation, without bitterness and without repining, from the first hour to the last.
—JOSEPH CONRAD, *The Mirror of the Sea*

When reverie and memory become confused, and fatigue and anguish set themselves up as lord and master, one must turn to all sorts of ruses so as not to abandon oneself to despair. My situation didn't differ greatly from that of a convict, locked in a dark dungeon, given food and drink at the most absurd and unpredictable times. I was scared of losing the notion of time.
—CRISTINA FERNÁNDEZ CUBAS, *The Year of Grace*

CONTENTS

THE ISLAND
OF LAST TRUTH

I don't remember who introduced me to Dr. Prendel. However, I do know that it was at the home of Martin Fleming, the psychiatrist, during a get-together of the faculty professors to celebrate his promotion from Assistant Dean to Dean, and I was immediately captivated by his reserved, taciturn attitude and the indifference with which he looked around him, as if he knew exactly what would happen and what would be said.

I also remember that it was Amy Fleming, Martin's wife, who told me of a certain legend that was circulating regarding Dr. Prendel. What's more, accidentally and not too long ago, Amy had met Prendel's dentist, and she'd told her that when he came to her clinic for the first time, she could clearly see by the state of his teeth that his diet had been irregular for a long period of time. This didn't prove but did strengthen the hypothesis that expert sailor Prendel had been shipwrecked years before, when his boat, the *Queen,* was attacked by a pirate ship. He'd lost his crew and his boat. He was left alive, a stroke of luck that, depending on the circumstances, is relative. The thing is Mathew Prendel disappeared for five years and at the time I was introduced to him, he'd been back in New York for four years, more or less. Since then, he'd been invited on more than one occasion to the parties the Flemings organized for one reason or another, parties he'd attended only rarely in the past. Everyone was dying to see a shipwrecked person up close. Dr. Prendel, however, had never accepted the invitation until that day, and after that day he never wanted to return.

According to those who had ever spent time with him, he was unrecognizable; not only his physical appearance, but above all his character. They also said that what had truly destroyed him wasn't the shipwreck, but the news on his return that his father had died alone, under the torrid Texan sun, sitting in the only chair on the sparse grass of his lawn. It seems his father had asked him many times not to let him die alone.

Among those who had known him best, there were those who said he wasn't even Prendel, but naturally no-one said this to his face and afterwards I never told him any of these rumors. He had enough misfortune, my poor doctor, being incapable of recognizing anyone from the past, as if being shipwrecked had erased his memory. Later I came to the conclusion that it wasn't amnesia, but defeat.

The doctor was a tall, thin man with large hands. Strong and attractive, without a doubt. Black hair already graying. A slight limp in his right leg. He was forty-five and lived on an "income." No one knew of what this income consisted. There were those who speculated about the possibility of the boat's insurers having paid him compensation of millions, but it was a baseless hypothesis. He never wanted to talk of his adventure to anyone. He did say that being shipwrecked was such an intimate experience that, as little modesty as one might have, it should be kept to oneself. Since his return to New York, Prendel was the favorite topic at these parties, and it seems that so he was once again after that day he accepted the invitation. I never went back myself.

It was easy to understand that, in reality, there was no-one left who really knew him: he'd lost his partner years before, his friends during the attack, his father in his absence. Mathew Prendel was alone, and furthermore, he was a loner, and maybe that was what made me feel an immediate complicity with him, the prodigious feeling of recognizing in his glance a demand equal to what I could give.

I hadn't heard anything about the whole shipwreck thing because I'd spent the last five years of my life falling apart in a marriage with no future and imparting classes in English literature at the University of Vienna, the city most closely resembling a postcard that I've ever seen. Among other things, I'd learned from the Viennese to discipline my impulsive, rash character and to adopt a reserved attitude even to what most stimulated my curiosity, for example a twenty-first-century pirate attack. When I was put before Prendel, nonetheless, I felt I was meeting Conrad or Stevenson. "You've got too much literature in your head," my grandfather would have said. Then added, "Watch that guy, little one, one can see in your eyes that you like him and there's something about him that doesn't suit you."

At no time did I doubt the legend. At no time did I think it might be a falsified story, a trivial anecdote embellished to the extreme and that, for example, Prendel could have lost his boat a few meters off the coast of Africa due to a more prosaic collision with a rock or another boat and later on, rumors had made it into a heroic exploit. I knew I couldn't ask him about it. As Amy said and everyone who ever came across him knew, Mathew Prendel had always maintained an absolute silence on the subject. So I sat by his side, drinking whiskey and listening to him explaining that African masks were in fact religious symbols with the function of stabilizing the lives of the villages. "Drink too much," my grandfather would have said, "and there's always a reason, Phoebe; people always drink the problems they can't solve in the form of alcohol."

Prendel had been a surgeon and later on, a professor at Columbia University. But his real passion was the sea. He was captain of a yacht. His hoarse, virile voice rang out above the others, or so I thought. I also thought that being a doctor would have helped him to survive the shipwreck. And captaining a yacht would have made him used to being alone. There are people equipped to be shipwrecked, people among whom I could never count myself, a professor of comparative literature who barely knew how to swim.

My friendship with Dr. Prendel bore fruit rapidly, perhaps because at a certain age the capacity for risk, if it has survived, turns out to be immense.

We were lovers for almost seven years. One of my aims was to endure longer than his shipwreck. As if some kind of rivalry or competition could be established with something like that. "You always want to defeat impossible opponents, Phoebe; opponents that aren't even there. You take after your mother." My victory has been bitter and, in truth, transient, because a "shipwreck" endures much longer than a shipwreck. It is like a lantern: it illuminates what you shine it on and the rest as well.

He asked me not to tell his story until after his death. But to tell it. "You who know literature, Dr. Westore, and have sailed with me, you may write it." We always spoke formally to each other; it was our game. And I promised him I would do it. It's absurd, but promises to the dead are pressing. Absurd because the dead can't care whether they are carried out. People usually fulfill promises to the dead with more zeal than those they make to the living. "I will write your story, Dr. Prendel," I assured him. "But beforehand you must tell it to me." After seven years of sleeping by his side, he hadn't told me a single detail. The surprise attack of the illness changed everything for him. "We know we have to die," he told me, "but we're not conscious of it until our hour comes." I remembered what my grandfather used to say: "Perhaps death is the best part of life. We'll have to wait and see."

THE SHIPWRECK OF MATHEW PRENDEL

Phoebe Westore

PART ONE

1.

The first incongruity that occupies Mathew Prendel's mind is thinking, just as he feels the roughness of the damp sand against his face, that he doesn't know if he is alive. It is pitch-black night, and he doesn't know if being alive is a stroke of luck either. He remembers the salty hell of the last few hours. How he has managed to arrive at a beach is unknown. He didn't even know there was an island at a distance he could cover swimming. The last coordinates taken with the GPS, which he'd noted meticulously on the map, fifteen minutes before the attack, gave a latitude and longitude of open sea many days' sailing from any point of dry land. They were more than eight hundred miles from the west coast of Africa. They'd left Jamestown a week before and were expecting to reach São Tomé, all going well and wind permitting, in eight or ten more days.

Katy Bristol was in the cockpit, gathering up the spinnaker. The wind, although light, had changed direction and the sail could no longer hold the course. Frank Czerny was in the cabin, making sandwiches for lunch. Mathew was steering. They were moving at a rate of six or eight knots, with a cross wind; a sufficient quantity of clouds, none threatening, defended them from the scorching heat of the midday Atlantic sun, at a point some five hundred miles southeast of the coordinates uniting the equator with the prime meridian. Katy put the spinnaker pole in its cover, went down to the cabin with the spinnaker folded up and back in the bag, made a joke about Frank's poor cooking in a very loud voice so Mathew would hear it too, and came back up top. She was carrying the binoculars. She was fond of using them even when there was nothing definite to be seen except the horizon which, despite always seeming much the same, changed according to the spirits of the person contemplating it. They were discussing the celebration they were going to have when they passed the equator. Katy was most insistent on the menu. She wanted them to prepare a special meal; she was tired of tins and sandwiches. All three were more or less in agreement that they had earned a celebration. As they were talking, Katy was looking through the binoculars. Suddenly, in a voice not altogether calm, she said:

"There's a yacht, port side. Three or four miles away. I can't see what flag they're flying. Looks big." The noise of the motor still hadn't reached them.

Mathew suspected that Katy was afraid. Some colleagues they'd met up with in Jamestown port on the island of Saint Helena had told them blood-curdling stories of pirates attacking sailors in the region, with a cruelty as unnecessary as it was unchanging. It was strange, because piracy was usually concentrated on the east coast of the African continent, but they assured them that at least one dangerous vessel which had caused the disappearance of more than one sailboat was operating in these waters. It wasn't their principal objective, because they made a living from contraband, but if they came across one, they plundered it.

Frank, who'd heard her, stuck his head out the companionway.

"Maybe we should change course. We could beat to windward and be out of sight. What do you think, Matt?"

But with the worst possible timing, Mathew didn't share his crewmember's fears. Doctor Prendel wanted to stick to the schedule they'd mapped out and now that they were taking a direct course towards their destination he didn't want to deviate from it. It wasn't the first time he had sailed in these waters, and he'd never had any run-ins with pirates, although he'd often heard about them.

"We'll keep going," he told them. It will be an annotation in the logbook: boat sighted at this time, latitude, longitude, that course. "Frank, how's that lunch coming?" The silence of his companions made him reflect. "All right," he gave in, "if we see them coming deliberately towards us, we'll change course."

But in sailing, as in life, you have to change course before hitting the obstacle. If you wait too long, you collide. It is as bad weather begins that you must lower the sails because when the storm is already upon you it is much more difficult and, at times, very risky if not impossible.

"They're coming directly towards us," informed Katy, who hadn't put down the binoculars, even to grab one of the sandwiches Frank had brought up. "Matt, they're coming head-on and there's no doubt they've spotted us. Either they have problems and need help or they'll make problems for us and the ones needing help will be us."

Mathew looked to where Katy was pointing. The binoculars were no longer necessary to see the boat. It had to be sixty foot. Bigger than the *Queen,* which was forty-two. It must be travelling with a considerable crew. However much they tacked, if the other boat chased them, they would catch them. Sails versus motor: it was obvious. The only solution—although calling it a solution was extravagantly optimistic—was to face them.

"Katy, go down and lock yourself in your cabin. Frank, look in the starboard trunk for an aluminum box, grab the pistol inside. Then lock yourself in as well."

"Pistol? Why do you have a weapon?"

"Does this seem like a good time to explain?" Dr. Prendel was a pragmatic man, decisive.

Katy hadn't moved. She wasn't planning to hide herself in the cabin. If it were necessary, she wanted to defend herself with her own hands. Frank told her that captain's orders couldn't be questioned. Katy answered that when your life is at risk, yes, they could. They argued for a few minutes before Prendel's impassive silence. It's easy for people to disagree when they are talking about death. Or when they are talking about life. It's easy for people to disagree.

"Doesn't matter. There's nothing to be done. We're done for. They're pirates," announced the captain. "They're predators. We'll be lucky to get away with our lives. But I'm not confident about it. At all."

Then Prendel thought that he shouldn't have changed the name of the boat, that the legend of bad luck pursuing vessels whose names had been changed was true and now being confirmed once again. Why couldn't he have a boat called *Mary*? How could memories weigh on him so much?

The captain turned the bow into the wind. Better to wait for them, show a total willingness to be plundered. And so he explained to his companions. There isn't only one way to be a victim, but Prendel was convinced that surrender was the optimum. He took off his gloves and leaned on the wheel to eat his cheese sandwich. He reflected that this was perhaps the last meal of his life. He looked at Katy and Frank and told them he was very sorry, very sorry to have involved them in this adventure whose close, tragic end could now be glimpsed. They answered that he shouldn't blame himself. Fear kept them tense and prudent.

"What can we give them? What are they hoping to find?" he asked out loud, but received no answer. Katy knew they were carrying nothing of value, except some money and their laptops. But that would seem like pure junk to pirates.

The *Queen* rocked lazily, calmly. The halyards slapped against the mast. The horizon line was broken only by the silhouette of the boat approaching them. Frank lit a cigarette.

"I'll have to resign myself to never having climbed the six hundred and ninety-nine steps of Jacob's Ladder," he said.

During the days they were docked in Jamestown port, Frank had tried to convince his companions to go see the island from above; to do so only required climbing the six hundred and ninety-nine steps of that narrow and steep staircase that ascended the mountain. Katy and Prendel kept putting him off and in the end they set sail without climbing it. Confessing that he would never satisfy that desire was an admission of death. "And you two? What did you not get to do?"

Dr. Prendel was calculating the time left before they were boarded. Five minutes? Ten?

"I don't know, Frank. If this ends here, I'll still want everything. I'm only thirty-six. You?" He turned to Katy.

"I'm thirty-eight, like Frank. I would like to have had a baby. But wouldn't you know it, now it would be left an orphan."

If they spoke so clearly of impending death, it is because they didn't believe in it. Believing in it might have saved them. Maybe, if they'd felt threatened up to that point, they would have sent an SOS by radio.

The appearance of the pirates was nondescript. No special mark or characteristic gave them away. Nevertheless, there was no doubt what they were. Five men on deck. Three black and two white. No visible weapons. The boarding was rapid. They pulled in alongside the *Queen* with the speed and efficiency of experience. They fixed cables to stern and bow. Two men came aboard the *Queen* and gave Prendel, who identified himself as captain, an order for him and the whole crew to throw themselves overboard. Seeing they spoke English, Prendel tried to talk to them.

"We have nothing of value," he told them.

The one who seemed to be calling the shots didn't delay in answering him.

"The boat's enough. Into the water."

"We'll die." It was Frank.

"Sooner or later, yeah," said another. And at that moment he pulled out a gun. They were getting impatient. "But if you prefer, we can kill you. Right now."

"At least let us lower the lifeboat," pleaded Katy.

The man who had just taken out his gun shot at the boat.

"No use now," he clarified needlessly.

Feeling scared and having nowhere to run to was a terrifying feeling. Mathew saw there was no way out, but he had to try.

"Look, I'm the owner of the boat, I mean, I'll jump overboard, OK? But let these two people off at a port or near some coast so they can swim to it."

"Are you negotiating with us? Do you think you're in a position to bargain?" He gave a signal. The one carrying the revolver shot and wounded Frank in the arm.

Desperate, Prendel took out his weapon. He only had time to shoot once and, unexpectedly, he gave it to one of those who had remained on the pirate ship. The man fell into the water and sank immediately. He didn't have to wait long for the pirates' response. Infuriated by the death of one of their own, they started shooting. As he threw himself overboard Mathew Prendel saw Frank and Katy gunned down. He swam furiously, conscious of the difficulty of avoiding the shots in that calm sea. However, the men didn't persist. Why waste bullets if Prendel would end up dying anyway? Of exhaustion or prey to some shark. Of hunger or thirst. Of desperation. Of loneliness. Drowned.

2.

Prendel doesn't feel the warm temperature of the water until he sees the pirate ship moving away. On the stern he can still make out the name, *Solimán*. Tugging his Swan 42; they had lowered her sails, defeated her. Even so, without meaning to, Prendel admires the line of her; he can tell himself he's had the boat of his dreams. He can tell himself he's made some of his dreams come true. He wonders if this is what counts, now that the moment has come to take stock.

He is surprised to feel cold just as the enemy leaves. He observes them. There's nothing else he can do. He knows that swimming is pointless. The only hope is that a boat may pass, but he knows that's unlikely; so much so that it is almost impossible. He is going to die. This idea causes him to shiver as he never has before. Within a short time he will have done two radical things: killed and died. About dying, the only thing that surprises him is the manner. About killing, everything. He would never have thought himself capable of killing anyone, even in extreme circumstances. Although he hasn't practiced for some time, being a doctor used to weigh heavily on him. So he had thought. And instead, he'd proven that his survival instinct functioned like the mechanism of a Swiss watch: silently, with precision. It wouldn't be useful to him anymore.

After a while, he sees them throw the bodies of Katy and Frank overboard. Mathew cannot forgive himself. He is going to die with the sorrow of having sacrificed his friends; the only ones he'd had in New York in all the years since his family left Baltimore and moved to the Big Apple for him to go to university. He remembers how he convinced them to join him: it was April and Prendel had just begun a sabbatical year. He'd gone looking for Katy and Frank at their nautical bookshop. They'd opened it six years before. Frank and Katy had been friends, and sometime lovers, since university. They'd both studied marine biology. It was lunchtime and he invited them to the place of their choice, although he already knew the answer if it were Frank who chose; he always suggested PJ Clarke's on the off chance he'd run into an old girlfriend of his, a tour guide he was still in love with.

"I have to tell you a dream which I've been going over in my mind for years and that now, finally, I can make come true," he told them en route from 57th to 55th Street. And little by little, while they each devoured one of those famous burgers, he seduced them. They would depart in May, to take advantage of favorable winds. They had already sailed on the *Queen* once and knew she was safe and comfortable. He would take care of the expenses. And the preparations. He'd requested a sabbatical year thanks to some stock market investments which had paid more than generous dividends. The lives they were leading would await them quietly. The two sales people they'd hired could mind the bookstore. They were talking about five months, six at the most.

"We have to do things in life that later on we'll want to remember. Look back and feel it's been worth it. Going over our history and feeling that it's not like anyone else's, it belongs to us, we invented it. We're young. We have to do it now. Now. I can't stand any more of this predictable life. Whatever we do, we'll end up dying. Worth doing what we want, isn't it?"

Prendel knew very well that everyone carries within himself a person who wants to break the routine, who wants to show that he is unique, who says there is only one life and it has to be seized. He also knew, as practicing medicine had allowed him to corroborate it on more than one occasion, that when a patient receives a terminal diagnosis, the first feelings to overwhelm him are sadness and regret for not having done anything special with the life he'd been given. And that was what counted.

Everyone carries within himself a person who believes he is better than their living self. Prendel addressed his friends' inner beings. And it was a good move, because they didn't know how to say no.

Now, on the contrary, he thinks it wasn't a good move but an unfair manipulation. Now that he is floating in an improvised cemetery he feels guilty. They should have fled as soon as Katy saw the boat. Or afterwards. They should have tried. He should have trusted Katy's intuition, or more simply, respected her fear. But fear, when it isn't contagious, is as untransferable as desire or disgust. Now the man has the sensation of having surrendered without resistance. He cannot manage to forgive himself, he isn't capable of telling himself he acted as he did because he thought it was the best way to stay alive. He feels stupid. He is angry at himself.

Many times he has feared dying in the sea, but he never imagined it would be this way. He'd feared storms and calms. Even feared the coast, when he'd seen it too close on stormy days. Feared darkness. How true it is that life surprises us even on the terrain we believe we have mastered most.

Since it seems worse to resign himself to dying motionless than to dying while moving, he begins to swim. But beforehand, and as though it matters at all, he calculates in which direction the nearest shore lies. He tries to remember: at the moment of the attack they were seven hundred miles north of Jamestown; Ascension Island was almost six hundred miles southeast of them; it's clear that the Ivory Coast is closer than Gabon, although the difference between dying six hundred or eight hundred miles off the coast is ultimately irrelevant. Finally he decides: north. He mocks his instinct for survival and settles for thinking that it gives meaning to his every stroke. Giving meaning to things is an inevitable part of human aspiration and now in his situation, alone as never before, if there is a predominant feeling it is, no doubt, that of being profoundly human.

Hours of sun remain. He will roast before he drowns. He would prefer to die in the water than in fire. He would prefer not to die at all. He tries to imagine he has the boat at his side and he is taking a dip, so he can enjoy one more moment before fear overcomes him. He takes an inventory. He is dressed in a red T-shirt, jeans, and non-slip boating shoes, a genuine irony if he thinks about how little he'll be able to walk. In his trouser pockets he is carrying a multiuse penknife and a watch with a compass, barometer, thermometer, alarm, and stopwatch on his wrist. He lost his revolver jumping into the water. His sunglasses are still hanging on a cord around his neck. He looks around.

Despite realizing it is one of the last images he will ever see, its beauty excites him. He would like to describe to someone the sensation of abundance he is feeling. Suddenly, he understands the here and now.

By night the water temperature will drop and he will experience slight hypothermia, not enough to kill him. He will die of thirst. A topical thought overpowers him: "Water, water everywhere!" But he knows very well he cannot give in to the temptation: if he drank seawater he would dehydrate much more rapidly. So what? he thinks. Strange, the instinct to cling to life even when you know you have no chance of survival. Under normal conditions it would take between three and five days to die of dehydration. Given the circumstances, it will all be much quicker. Sometimes he had wanted to die. Now he realizes, no. Never. He didn't know then what it meant to face your own death.

He keeps swimming. He is not a great swimmer. He doesn't breathe well, he tires. He does the dead man's float again. Face up. Then he relaxes into the fetal position. Luckily, from time to time a cloud blocks the sun. He looks at the time. Four o'clock. The time has passed quickly. His hands and feet are wrinkled. His skin itches. He feels a cramp in his legs. He would like to have a nap. He would like to have something to eat. Most of all he would like to have something to drink. Impossible. He is in the corridor of death. He touches the knife in his pocket. The wait is unbearable. He could use it and end it all. Life is not a decision. Death, yes. He grabs the knife, opens it. Vein at the wrist? Jugular? He takes a deep breath.

He can't do it. Kill himself. Let death come and take him. Make it hard for her. He has no intention of making her a gift of his life. What has he been thinking? Mathew Prendel is a survivor. This isn't the first time death has been near. On more than one occasion, when he has distanced himself from the crowds of people that gather on land, when he has gone off to find himself, to feel the freedom of not being in the place assigned to him and is accountable only to himself, the price has been almost losing his life. Time and again he has proven that the only victory the sea concedes is survival. Until now. This will be his final crossing. Now he is alone forever. There is a bitter sting in the thought that no one will be able to feel his disappearance at the moment it strikes. He has been able to mourn the deaths of Katy and Frank. He has accompanied them. He accompanies them still now as he thinks of them, lifeless.

Dr. Prendel thinks of his widowed father, there in Georgetown, that lost Texas town where many well-heeled retirees live.

"Texas? Why are you going to Texas? Aren't you happy in New York? You can live with me, if you like."

But the man preferred the climate of the South, the calm of a small town.

"If your mother were still alive, I would stay here. She couldn't bear small places, she adored cities, and New York more than any other. Remember when we left Baltimore, even her personality changed! But I feel lonely, son; you have your work and a lot of the time you go off to those remote seas for months at a time, and I don't know what you're looking for so far from our country. You're away more than you're here, and I feel lonely, son, and there are many people my age there, people who have lost their spouse, people looking for meaning in the final years of life, you'll understand when you grow old."

But Mathew Prendel will never grow old. And his father will never be as alone as he is right now, at six in the evening on the day Mathew's slow death begins.

It will take his father months to realize that they won't see each other again. It will destroy his heart and he knows this. He will say: "How many times did I tell him to forget about all those adventures, settle down, how many times did I tell him it would end badly if he continued like that."

His father is seventy-one years old. His mother would be sixty-one, if she were still alive. Death didn't pay attention to the age difference. It took her five years before in less than a month. The liver.

Mathew was an only child. He'd have liked to have had a sibling. He thinks it's safe to say they'd be together now, and this thought consoles and distresses him at the same time.

Many times he has felt sadness imagining his father alone, in the small living-dining room of his house. Sitting on the crimson plastic sofa, the television on at a deafening volume. Dozing and taking gulps of coffee served in one of those cups you get with points from yogurt or paper napkins. His shirt and trousers freshly washed, but with old stains on them. And it is curious, because now he feels an even more profound pity for him. A pity, he supposes, that has to do with knowing how alone he is leaving him while his father still thinks he can count on his company.

3.

Night has fallen. It is two o'clock in the morning. He is exhausted. He is cold and afraid. He hadn't been afraid while it was light. Seeing his body through the water helped him to be sure there was nothing worrisome nearby. The sea, when everything is dark, is like an immense animal with black skin moving restlessly as it sleeps and may wake up any moment. He has been swimming for hours, with brief interruptions to do the dead man's float. Dead man's float, what an expression for a moment like this. He would swell up and the fishes would eat him. Better that than being cremated or buried. He'd always thought he'd like his ashes to be scattered at sea. The sea, the tomb. Now they wouldn't be ashes but all of him. Wasn't that what you wanted? Now you have it. He smiles. He hasn't lost his sense of humor. Or maybe this is what death is: hoping, smiling, despairing, understanding nothing while on the verge of understanding everything.

His mother had been buried. Afterwards, for a long time, Prendel had nightmares in which bodies emerged with huge worms slithering through them. His mother, unlike his father, always told him: "It's good that you go all over the world, that you value things that aren't bought or sold or measured, that you don't always have your feet on the ground, that you start over again." Who knows if he'll find her again. Who knows if there is a place where the dead reunite to go over their lives, comment on them, project them like a film. Forward, rewind, pause, slow motion, freeze image.

The cold has relieved the sensation of thirst. But his head hurts. He knows that's normal. The first symptoms of dehydration. Increased heartbeat and respiration. Spasms, nausea. And afterwards he'll have hallucinations. He'll see an island, a boat, he'll hear voices. Mirages. He'll see salvation.

He keeps going. Very slowly. It's difficult for him to move his arms. He can hardly feel his hands or feet. He orientates himself by the stars. He keeps swimming towards the continent. In the depths of his heart he believes that maybe he'll get to a shipping lane for merchant ships or oil tankers; maybe some boat will change direction for an unforeseen reason, a breakdown perhaps. In any case, he is still mocking his survival instinct.

Sailing means knowing where we are, where we have come from, and where we are going. Therefore it is perhaps more difficult to sail than to live. Right now, Prendel can calculate where he is. He can calculate the speed at which he has been swimming, his approximate direction, and the amount of time he has spent in the water. He is sailing without a vessel. This is what will kill him. Although he is lost, he hasn't lost himself. He is a good sailor. Frank and Katy knew that, and so they had set sail with him. They had trusted too much in his skill. Or perhaps they didn't figure that sooner or later the sea kills you; the only difference is that if you are a good sailor, you know where you are at the moment of dying.

Mathew rebukes himself for having thought that things happen to other people. Everyone wants to choose. Loneliness won't happen to me, failure won't happen to me, not ruin or sickness or pirates. Pain, hunger, the ending of a love story won't happen to me. But it has to happen to someone.

The ending of a love story happened to him. Worse than that. He remembers Mary Stradform with a mixture of nostalgia and rage. Professor of pediatric surgery during his final year of medical school. They fell in love after a few classes. Contrary to habit, he asked her out for coffee. She said yes. They had coffee. The following day they woke up together in Mary's flat. He remembers the white cotton sheets and on top, her underwear, midnight blue. The salty taste of her skin, so similar to the taste of the waves. Loving her gave meaning to his life. He introduced her to his parents. He went to live with her. First and last love.

When they'd been together a little over two years, that operation happened. A little girl seven years old, a transplant, a disaster. Mary Stradform, prestigious surgeon, drowning in anxiety. She lost her touch. I didn't have the hands for the operating theater any more, she'd say. It was my fault, she'd say. The little girl would have survived. I didn't do it right, she'd repeat. I killed her. She'd killed her. And Mary Stradform committed suicide. She disappeared forever. She left him alone. But not as alone as he finds himself now, facing his own death, rather alone in a different solitude, the one felt only after the death of others.

Afterwards, to avenge Mary, to find peace, to get even with himself, and even with her, Dr. Prendel started to operate on seven-year-old girls. He specialized in pediatric surgery. To save himself and save her. Not long afterwards, however, his firm resolve began to waver and he sought refuge as a professor at Columbia University. He'd built up a good rèsumè and they accepted it without objections. He never picked up a scalpel again. He didn't want this godlike power, to give and take life. He wanted to be responsible only for his own. Many lamented his resignation. Prendel was a great professional. An honest person. Also an unsociable man with the soul of an adventurer. Few had understood his flight.

But Dr. Prendel hadn't fled. You don't flee from something when you go searching for something else, and he'd seen that life could be something else. That there were other possibilities. Sailing was a way of finding himself, of knowing what he wanted. Knowing what he didn't want. And now, despite the cold, his wrinkled, cramped hands and feet, physical and mental exhaustion, imminent death, Mathew Prendel knows that there are many things he doesn't want in his life from before. He is sure that rather than return to it, he prefers to move forward, directly to the destiny reserved for him at the bottom of the sea, with Katy, Frank, and darkness.

The darkness begins to fade. The dawn's first light illuminates the horizon. Prendel makes out the round profile of the world once more. Life becomes reality. The night has been an unfortunate parenthesis. The day is not a parenthesis, but it too is unfortunate. It was not a nightmare. The lightbulbs the moon had been lighting in the water all night disappear. Now everything is gray. It will only be an instant. The sun will not take too long to rise. It will be the second day out of a maximum of three. He gulps a little water. Bad move. But his thirst is becoming unbearable. He has no point of reference to know where he is. He can no longer calculate how he is advancing. He doesn't want to wait for death. He is impatient to meet it. Why are no sharks attacking him? If he cuts himself, maybe his blood will attract some. But he is afraid of being devoured by a beast. He fears the bite, the pain, the horror. During the night he suffered a shock: something brushed against him while he was almost dozing, doing the dead man's float and he came to violently. He has lost his sunglasses. By night, he didn't think it important, but now he thinks he should have paid more attention, should have tried to find them, get them back. He also thinks he shouldn't be hard on himself, shouldn't reproach himself, what he is doing is already enough. But that's always been his style, blaming himself, suffering, asking too much of himself. Perhaps because of this, sailing alone had been good for him, to gain an understanding of the fine but key difference between blame and responsibility. One is not to blame for breaking a halyard at the least opportune time but is responsible for not having replaced it in time. One is not to blame for failing to take down the sails at the right time but is responsible for not having followed the old adage: "the first moment you think you should take down the sails is the time to do it; afterwards it's already too late." On land, on the other hand, other people's stares return an image filtered through a judgment that much of the time implies guilt. Wanting to share it with Frank and Katy, rather than feeling responsible, he felt guilty once again.

He shouts. He hadn't thought of doing so until now. He shouts, "Help." Maybe the wind will carry his cry to a boat. Desperate, he shouts. He should have done so by night. Why hadn't he thought of it?

He hadn't thought of it because it's absurd. There is no boat to be seen. And faced with miles of sea and more sea, his voice seems ridiculous.

He shouts, shouts, shouts. Help. Help.

He knows it's pointless. But how many times do we do pointless things?

4.

He sees an island. He was prepared for it to happen. But seeing it, he can't help but feel a happiness as previously unknown as this piece of land ahead of him.

He doesn't know how much time has passed. He isn't sure. He had let go completely. He was no longer hoping for anything. Now, however, he has strength again. As if he has just abandoned the *Queen*. He has to give his body precise instructions, which it doesn't obey at first. He has to tell his body not to swim, something his brain doesn't understand, no; he has to tell it to move his arms and legs as if they were blades.

As he moves forward, he wonders how it is possible his eyes haven't been burned. His lips are cut and contact with the salty water stings. How far is it? A mile? Maybe less. Definitely less. How is it possible? He's sure that there was no island or islet on the nautical map. Or he didn't remember it . . . but that's impossible . . . there was nothing but water.

And then experience, knowledge, and reality make an appearance and Dr. Prendel, dying, realizes that the time for hallucinations has come, little time is left to him before he loses his senses and he can stop struggling. And this thought tires, and at the same time, relaxes him.

He stops swimming and loses consciousness.

Later, completely disorientated, the first incongruity that occupies Mathew Prendel's mind is the thought, just as he feels the roughness of the damp sand against his face, that he doesn't know if he is alive. It is pitch-black night, and he doesn't know if being alive is a stroke of luck either. He remembers the salty hell of the last few hours. How he has managed to arrive at a beach is unknown. It wasn't a mirage.

With an effort he drags himself along. He moves away from the water. Once again, he loses consciousness.

* * *

The next thing Dr. Prendel feels is someone's hands holding his head. Although he doesn't have the strength to open his eyes, the doctor knows it is day by the light reaching him through his closed eyelids. The other person tries to give him water to drink. Prendel is frightened. Where is he?

"Drink, drink," the person tells him. He speaks his language. "You'll survive," he says. "Don't worry. You'll survive. Drink."

Will he survive?

Dr. Prendel drinks. Very slowly. He is no longer thirsty. Or he doesn't feel it. He only wants to sleep. Forever. In fact, when he has drunk a little, the voice says, "Rest." Afterwards he hears some footsteps moving away, then nothing.

He doesn't wake until night. He opens his eyes. It's difficult to focus. The first thing he sees is the fire beside him. Then a man. He deduces that this is the man who saved him.

He hears the sound of the waves nearby. He lifts his head a little and checks that, in fact, the shore is just a few feet away. Prendel is covered with a jacket. He has dry clothes and feels warm. He throws the cover off. He tries to sit up but fails. He is very weak. He remains lying on the ground.

"My name is Nelson Souza," the other's voice sounds in the darkness. Prendel guesses that he is a white man. Against Prendel's wishes, this fact unsettles him. "You should eat and drink something. Here." He passes him a cup of water. And something solid. "It's fish," he tells him.

Prendel accepts; he's too weak to ask or question anything. He drinks anxiously; now he is thirsty. Then he eats. The fish is hard and rubbery.

"Thank you." His voice surprises him: he hasn't heard it for many hours. It comes out weak. "Where are we?" he asks. Now, he sits up little by little. He feels sick. He feels strange. Shouldn't he be dead?

"On a tiny island in the middle of the Atlantic," the man answers. "Southeast of the Gulf of Guinea."

Prendel thinks that's impossible.

"We can't be," he says.

Souza doesn't answer. Now he is pouring a hot drink, in the same cup as before.

Prendel looks around him, but can't manage to make anything out. Perhaps some shadows. The worst has passed; nevertheless, he is uneasy.

"Are you from here?" Prendel asks Souza.

"As much from here as you are."

"So it's deserted, the island?" Prendel, despite his weakness, realizes he's asked a stupid question.

"Completely," Souza informs him. "We've been shipwrecked on a minuscule, deserted island.

"We have?" With an effort Prendel swallows a last bit of fish.

"I haven't been here much longer than you," Nelson informs him.

Prendel sees that the man is wearing a bandage on his ankle.

"You're injured," he states more than asks.

"Yes, from a gunshot."

The image of the man falling over the side of the pirate ship appears instantly in Prendel's head. He swallows. His life has been saved only to lose it again. It couldn't be any other way, he thinks. Life, sooner or later, is lost. "A gunshot?"

"Your shot, yes." He looks the pirate in the eyes. Prendel thinks he has a frank gaze. Too frank for his taste.

"I thought I'd killed you," clarifies Prendel, while he feels overwhelmed by a strange relief, and thinks how reversible everything in life is, even the most extreme things. He was convinced he'd killed a man and was on the verge of dying. Instead, neither the one nor the other. For that reason hope is the last thing one loses, he thinks; life has so much more imagination than human beings, is never, even in the face of the most conclusive proof, predictable or definitive.

"No, as you can see."

"Why didn't you raise the alarm? Why didn't you go back to your friends' boat?"

"They're not my friends," Souza clarifies, laconically. Then he sees Prendel looking at the revolver he is wearing inside his trousers, fastened to his belt.

"You've got nothing to be afraid of. Things have changed now."

Prendel thinks that indeed things have changed and men are who they are depending on who is around them.

"You mean we're not enemies." Prendel clearly sees that the other man holds considerable power. The other man is himself plus his gun. Might is a sad but infallible way of constituting a majority.

"Here we're nothing but survivors." Souza, who was standing, squats down opposite him and stirs the branches; the fire revives. Prendel takes advantage of the light and looks at his surroundings. The outline of a low mountain is drawn against the full moon.

"How do you know there's no one else on the island?"

"When day breaks you'll see why. It's barely six or seven square kilometres. We're lucky there's water, plants, trees, fish. Enough to survive a good while, I think."

"Why did you save me?" Dr. Prendel, who has saved so many lives, doesn't understand why a man has saved his.

"You don't kill a man who may be useful to you." Souza stares at Prendel.

"But you know that he who saves another man's life makes himself responsible for him until the end of his days . . . "

Nelson Souza interrupts him.

"If I'd known that, I'd have left you to die. Anyway, who knows if we'll manage to get out of here some day."

"Well,, maybe some boat, sooner or later . . . "

"No sooner or later, no boat, no nothing. This island is a long way from all the commercial routes. In fact, it's a miracle our boat was so close . . . but that's another story. We're scarcely a few hours' swim from the place of attack. You were swimming in circles for sure. And I . . . well, you get here faster when you know where you're going."

"How did you know where . . . ?" Prendel begins to ask, but Souza interrupts him once more.

"The thing is no oil tankers or merchant ships or yachts pass anywhere near here. Where were you going? To São Tomé? You should have been sailing closer to the coast, but I imagine you wanted to avoid the traffic of the big ships or wanted to take advantage of the wind. The only ones who come close to here from time to time are the ones that belong to *Solimán*."

Prendel remembers the boat moving away, the name painted on the stern.

"They could have rescued you. If they find me, they'll kill me for sure, but you . . . "

"They think I'm dead. Drowned at the bottom of the Atlantic. And that's what they have to think. You're either with them or you're against them."

"I don't know if I understand."

"You don't need to understand," says Nelson Souza, while he presses on his injured ankle with a grimace of pain. "All you have to know is that if you try to make signals from the island so they find us . . . I'll have to kill you. It will be me who decides when and how we leave here, is that clear?"

Prendel nods because he realizes that the tone Souza is using leaves no room for questions or complaints. He is too tired to argue. He looks around him. All his priorities are changing. What was important before is no longer so. What wasn't, will be. A man doesn't know what it costs to revise the list of his values until he has to do it. He had been somewhat used to it, given the changes involved in leaving the land to go to sea, but . . . this was totally different. This was land in the middle of the sea. It was like sailing without managing to move from the place. It was terrible. He looks back at the man in front of him.

Nelson Souza is thin but strong, tall, with thick black hair. Now he's got a beard of a few days. Prendel reckons that Souza is about his own age. He tries to ignore the threat. He doesn't want to ask the reason for it; he knows he won't answer. He points at his wound.

"It hurts, right? If you'll allow me, I can take a look at it. I'm a doctor. A doctor with no instruments or medication."

"A doctor? Hey, then I did well in saving you. A doctor and a pirate: clearly all we're missing is a priest and we could be a bad joke, couldn't we?" Nelson smiles. Prendel imitates him. Souza keeps talking. "I have some medicine. A first-aid kit. I've been taking antibiotics."

"The surprised look on Prendel's face forces Nelson to give some explanation.

"I didn't fall into the water empty-handed. I fell pre-pared. I was hoping to fall. It was lucky you shot me. Thanks."

Prendel smiles, though with bitterness. He misses Frank a lot, a guy who liked this kind of situation. Two men alone, shipwrecked on a desert island, and one thanks the other for having fired a bullet into his ankle. Frank was a guy who liked westerns and war films.

"Move your leg closer to the fire." He says it in an authoritative tone. The other man obeys. Mathew uncovers the wound and examines it. "It should have had stitches. Not now, it's too late."

He is lying on the sand. Prendel feels the dampness of the ground. He is exhausted. He looks at the time. It is two o'clock in the morning, but in the situation he's in, time means nothing.

"Too much light, for my liking. I like to sleep in the dark," he comments calmly, almost as if this were any other night. At the moment, he is more struck by his having survived than by being in an open-air prison.

"The firelight will go out on its own, shortly. The moonlight . . . will take a little longer."

Souza has spent almost two days alone. He wasn't expecting anyone. Prendel gathers that his presence is a relief, and for that reason he wasn't capable of letting him die. He closes his eyes and hears Souza going away. His footsteps, slightly unequal in intensity because of his wound, move away surely over the sand. Prendel remembers Frank and Katy. He realizes he should have ordered them to throw themselves overboard the instant the pirate demanded it. Now he knows they too would have been saved. And having them with him would have given him peace. Nelson Souza had saved his life, yes, but he can't forget where he comes from. In any case, he has said it clearly: he doesn't plan on killing a man who might be useful to him. But he will kill him if he tries to give signal any ship that might appear on the horizon. Until when?

5.

Two days later, Prendel still feels weak, but he is able to stand up. He has slept, he has rested, and he has recuperated, thanks to Souza's help. His eyes run over his surroundings: he sees the whole island in all its negligible size. Or almost all. The expanse of fine white sand broken by sticks, algae, all types of shells, where he has lain for so many hours is bordered on one end by the Atlantic and on the other by intricate vegetation extending to the foot of a forested mountain, which, according to what Souza has explained to him, ends in a cliff on the other side. Going up isn't easy, but it's worth the effort, because on the top you can find bird's eggs. Souza, who was standing next to him when he awoke, tells him that on the other side of the mountain there is a minimal strip of sand, which disappears when the tide comes in and can only be reached on foot at low tide from the western side of the island, or by swimming.

Nelson Souza is carrying a medical kit under his arm. He starts unwinding the bandage on his leg. Prendel watches, carefully cleans the skin, tells him it will scar in a few days; he gives instructions on how to keep the injury clean and all the while tries to overcome the hatred rising within him; a hatred mixed with gratitude for having saved his life.

"Where did you get the medical kit?" Prendel wants to know. Souza doesn't respond. From a pouch he takes out a tin, a cup, a couple of hooks with fishing lines, a water bottle, and a lighter. He leaves it on the ground, beside the medical kit.

"You'll need them," he announces and starts walking. He is limping. "We have work to do," he says.

Mathew Prendel doesn't yet dare ask where this arsenal of objects has come from. He follows Souza.

"Work?" Prendel looks around him. "Is there something lacking on this island?" His sarcasm, as usual, is closely linked to rage, to pain.

The humidity is suffocating. He looks at his watch: it is ten in the morning and the heat is already unbearable.

"I have to show you the island, we have to establish some rules of coexistence," says Nelson. "We'll be spending some time here. It will be better to be clear on some rules."

Rules? Prendel waits for clarification. Rules?

"Are rules necessary between two men on a desert island?"

Nelson answers: "Yes, they are. Over there, on the other side, I have my hut. It's important we mark out territories; I presume you understand."

His tone is authoritative. It is clearly an order. Prendel thinks Souza doesn't trust him. He also thinks it's better not to argue with an armed man, at least for the moment, so he immediately says yes, that seems like a good idea.

"In my territory there is nothing that might interest you. In other words, you have no reason to enter it, under any pretext. However, I will need to come here, to look for water and food."

Prendel doesn't feel comfortable with the idea that only his part of the island is to be shared but while this sensation is coming over him, he realizes that this desire for ownership is stupid in a situation in which all that matters is survival. He is thirsty and hungry. Hot and scared. Does he need a piece of island just for himself? Instead he says: "I too should have a territory, a place where you can't go."

He says this but he probably thinks: Am I aware that I am shipwrecked? Do I realize my friends have been assassinated, the *Queen* stolen from me, I've almost been killed and the guy whom it's fallen to me to live with on this island is one of those bastards who destroyed my life? An impulse that doesn't even reach his body pushes him towards Nelson. Nevertheless, Prendel stands still, not knowing what to expect.

Nelson shrugs and starts walking. Prendel follows him. Nelson moves deeper into the vegetation at the foot of the mountain. He parts branches with his arms. He fills his water bottle with the water accumulated on some leaves among the vines.

"With the rain in the area and condensation, we're not going to be thirsty. It would be a pain to have to desalt the seawater." Prendel imitates him. He drinks a sip. The water is good, warm but good. "There at the foot of the mountain, you'll see there are some entrances into the rocks and in some cavities little puddles form. These entrances, by the way, will be your only possible shelter when the rain is torrential."

Had some ship been wrecked on the part of the island Souza considers his? Is that where he got all these things from? The cap, the small axe hanging from his belt, the revolver. Why is Souza helping him? How can he be helpful?

Prendel doesn't ask questions. He knows they'll get no response. And even if they did, Prendel doesn't ask questions because that humid heat fills his lungs so he is incapable of doing anything but pant. He stops looking at Nelson, who is clearing the path, and looks astonished at his surroundings. He sees flowers of unbelievable color combinations, insects that look like plants and plants that look like insects. After spending so much time in the sea, looking at the immensity of the horizon, it seems strange to use his capacity to see at close range, once again, to focus his eyes on small objects, and he thinks that this is one of the great differences between life on land and life on the sea. On land things are always up close, often too close, and there is a lack of perspective, distance, relativity. He thinks this and says it to Nelson.

Nelson stops, turns round, takes off his cap, wipes the sweat of his brow, looks at Prendel with expression of incredulity.

"This is what you're thinking about, now, as we struggle to walk under this murderous heat? Seriously?"

He puts his cap back on and continues walking. Prendel turns around and turns back to the beach. He doesn't have to stay behind him. He'll discover for himself what there is to be discovered.

With the knife he cuts a pair of vines, one large branch, not too thick, and some palm leaves. Once on the beach, he ties the vine around the leaves, joins them to the branch, and is satisfied, when he sticks the construction into the ground, that it holds up and works for the purpose he made it: Prendel has made a sunshade. When the sun goes down he will begin building a shelter. He also wants a place where Nelson won't have access, his own place.

Nelson, who appears a little while later, watches Prendel, who is sitting in the shade, from afar. Afterwards he comes closer.

"I've put together material for several days," he says. "There," and he points to the wood—"you'll find all manner of worms, lizards, snakes, you'll see. Some bugs you can eat yourself, and others you can use them as bait for the fish. They'll bite, for sure. And speaking of bites, be careful with the poisonous snakes."

"How do I distinguish them?"

"You can't."

Prendel nods. And Nelson adds: "Another thing: Don't come into my territory, don't come near me, because I won't hesitate to shoot."

"I don't understand," admits Prendel. "You saved my life, we're on a desert island, alone, we don't have much chance of getting out of here. Shouldn't we join forces?"

"Doctor, it's better that you don't think. Obey and everything will be easier."

"Clearly your reasons are more powerful than mine," says Prendel, while he watches Souza walk away, his feet sinking into the sand just as Prendel's hopes have been sinking.

6.

After the first days of his arrival on the island, Prendel etches a calendar on the side of a rock. Although he doesn't want to dwell on it, being shipwrecked might last longer than his watch battery. According to his calendar, it is six weeks since he arrived. If the attack on the *Queen* was the 14th of June, that means it is now the end of July, the 30th or 31st if his calculations are correct. He hasn't seen Souza for forty-five days. He doesn't know if the man comes into his part of the island by night, while he is sleeping, or if he hasn't come back since the last time he saw him. Sometimes he thinks that Souza may have had an accident, that maybe Souza has died from drowning or a snakebite. His revenge is not to invade his territory. If he's been injured, all the worse for him.

The doctor has been busy also in the construction of a hut made of twigs as thick as branches and leaves, plentiful materials in the forest and subject to being manipulated by him, with no tools available. I have made myself a cell, he thinks. I live inside a closed cage, in an open-air prison. The floor is a rectangle. The walls, a little taller than him. The roof is made of leaves sewn together with thin vines. The door of the cell faces the forest. That way he is protected from the wind and what's more he feels safer. If Nelson approaches, he will make noise.

Now that he has at last finished the shelter, he feels exhausted and looks at the structure with a mixture of pride, which he admits with a gesture, and shame, because he has the feeling of having imitated the books he has read, having acted like a textbook shipwreck, instead of thinking seriously about what he should do in his situation. It's done, he says out loud. He thinks that an unusually strong wind could bring the whole thing down. It's done, he repeats. He believes that this way he'll defend himself better from insects, from little animals, from whatever there is. He thinks that a man always wants a roof, that what he covers himself with matters more than what he treads on. It's eight o'clock in the evening. He had calculated that he was going to finish today and he has prepared himself a kind of extraordinary dinner. For a moment, it crossed his mind to invite Souza. But then he immediately changed his mind and besides he wouldn't have known how to contact him. He lights a fire near his cell and cooks the shellfish he has caught. He goes over the time that has passed. He realizes that for the first two weeks, despite Souza's warnings, he'd been scanning the horizon, to try to detect the passing of a ship. By the third week, perhaps convinced that they really were alone in the middle of the Atlantic and no-one would come to save them, he'd begun to pay more attention to his needs. Almost without noticing, in that time he has learned how to collect water, catch lobster at low tide, select worms and lizards, to make a good fire, to find turtle eggs, and he knows how to distinguish certain herbs. He's discovered, without wanting to, that some have the effect of a laxative. He knows how to exploit the tender heart of some palm trees to eat. He has tried various fruits. He's found some entrances in the rock of the mountain. He has learned to recognize different types of silence, always mixed with the buzzing of the insects, the sound of the sea, the song or cry of a bird. All the silences allow him to listen to himself. He can't say that he has become accustomed to this life, but neither can he say that he is suffering. Is this victory? Adaptation? In what does a man's triumph consist? In surviving or escaping? He feels that nothing and no one is waiting for him in New York. Mary is a ghost from the past, Katy and Frank mean pain and guilt. He is conscious that his life had reached a pivotal moment, one of those moments in which things can go one way or another and are in no hurry. When he left New York it had been a while since he had found meaning in anything he did. Was that all there was to life? Nothing more? Just a series of anecdotes related to money, culture, work relations, and personal success? Was it possible that life was only this waiting to see if something happened? Could it not consist of making something happen? What could provoke someone to wish to return to a place that they'd wanted to leave? Nostalgia for comfort? Fear? Habit? The only thing that worries him is his father. Mathew remembers the last time he visited him in Georgetown he had helped him to paint the fence. The man seemed sad and tired. He'd said to Mathew, in that voiceless voice that was all he had left: "What I want is that you don't leave me to die alone, Mathew. Your mother wouldn't have wanted it either. Your mother was lucky that we stayed with her. Remember, Matt, the way your mother used to laugh, even at the end?" He always asked Matt about his mother's laugh, so characteristic and contagious, rising in a crescendo. His father would die still in love with her; he'd had the luck of finding love.

He also thinks that he has not yet despaired and that maybe it has been thanks to the building of the hut. He thinks that perhaps now the anguish will begin. There is no shipwreck until someone realizes you are ship-wrecked. There is no drowning in the water until the air is gone.

Or perhaps the tragedies one imagines at a distance turn into nothing more than adverse situations when they come closer. We never know what we will be capable of; that's unknowable.

* * *

Prendel is under the shade, opposite his shelter. He knows it is impossible to do anything before the sun goes down; the heat will dehydrate him. He has learned to stay still and wait for the day to pass. Strange what one learns when one must be still. Sometimes he feels he is a sick person, immobilized in bed, in a hospital, in front of a window. And then, despite everything, he prefers being ship-wrecked, He imagines he is sailing, he remembers the dead hours he spent on the windless sea, so many times, waiting for the slightest breeze to get the feeling of moving. The island is a sailboat without sails, a sailboat with its keel caught, a sailboat with a permanent invisible anchor.

"I see you've managed to drive stakes in the sand, you've had to bury them deep, right? If not, they don't last."

Souza has suddenly appeared, he's come out of the woods. He is wearing a cap and has another in his hand.

"Take it," he tells him.

Prendel grabs the cap, sees that it bears the brand of an alcoholic beverage, thanks him, and puts it on. It has a good visor. What a rest for his eyes. He misses his sunglasses.

"I thought maybe you'd died," Prendel says to him. "I was about to come to see you. I climbed all the way up there," and he points to the mountaintop, "but the rock juts out so far it is impossible to see what's beneath. All you can see is the sea."

"You were right not to come. We were clear on that."

"Just one thing—will it be long before we can leave here? Try to, I mean."

Mathew wonders what system Nelson Souza must have come up with to keep watch over his movements. He also thinks that Souza does not need to watch him. He represents no danger, and if he approaches his area, he kills him and that's that.

"Enough time has to pass for them to forget me."

"But that's absurd!" Prendel stands up, goes over to Nelson, who puts his hand on his revolver, a gesture that doesn't go unnoticed by Mathew. "We could try to build a kind of raft and go look for the oil tankers' shipping lanes."

"You've seen a lot of movies, haven't you?" Nelson looks scornfully at the hut built by Prendel. "Do you really think we'd get anywhere with a raft? Do you really think we wouldn't be shipwrecked less than ten meters from here? You seriously think there's a chance of getting out of this prison other than with a real boat?"

"Do you have a better plan? Eh?"

Souza has started to walk straight towards the woods and Prendel follows him, shouting.

"Eh? Do you have a better plan? Do you?"

Souza stops, comes back, looks Prendel in the eye and says: "I'm only going to say this once. Yes, I have a plan and I will explain it to you when it suits me. I'm in charge here and that's how it will be as long as I'm alive and I plan to stay alive for all the time it takes to get out of this hole, understand?"

Prendel thinks it strange that Nelson has said the island is a hole. A well, yes. This means that Nelson is just as desperate as him. Prendel would attack him but he knows he is bound to lose. He realizes that he will have to come up with a plan for himself alone; first to steal Nelson's authority, then to leave the island. Looking resigned, he asks: "OK. And how do you work out the time it will take them to forget you, your friends?"

"They're not my friends. And I'll know, for sure."

Dr. Prendel says nothing else. He observes Souza from behind; would this be a good moment to attack him? No, no, it must be well thought-out. He cannot act on impulse. He will only have one chance. And if he fails, Souza will have realized that Mathew is not prepared to obey and will not hesitate to do away with him. He sees Souza go towards the trail they have forged in the vegetation of the forest. He follows him for a moment or two. He studies his speed. Despite the limp, Nelson walks quickly, he is agile. He is wearing his shirtsleeves rolled up, the knife open in his hand and a revolver on his belt. This man saved him only to bury him alive. Incomprehensible. Maybe he's crazy. And he might make Mathew crazy too. What conditions are necessary for a sane man to go out of his mind?

Prendel approaches the shore. He wets his feet, hands,

splashes his face. He looks towards the horizon and thinks it's really true that for a sailor, the feeling of having arrived isn't always tied to the fact of touching land.

PART TWO

1.

Mathew didn't tell me his story until we'd almost arrived at the end of our own. Seven years gave me time to see him looking lost again and again, and every one of those times I'd been on the verge of asking him to confide in me even a little of his suffering. I longed to know the details of what happened, I wanted to comfort him about it all, whatever it might be, but I knew it was a touchy subject and I sensed there were some experiences that he in no way wanted to relive.

Prendel wasn't happy at my side. He wasn't a happy man, although he was master of his time, his decisions, his life. There was nothing that he couldn't allow himself and what's more, he was very generous. I never had a desire that he didn't try to fulfill. When he gave presents, however, he appeared to be paying a debt. He seemed absent. Perhaps it was true that his father's death had deeply disturbed him. Although he never spoke of him. He didn't have a single photograph of him, it was as if the old man had never existed. In fact, it was as if nothing from his life before the shipwreck had existed. He didn't mix with anyone, fled from people, wanted to be alone. With me or alone. He liked to travel. And sail, of course. He'd bought a boat and named it *Lisbon*. When he told me his story I understood why.

He hadn't wanted to go back to giving classes. He said

he didn't need the money and, besides, he had nothing to teach, that, on the contrary, he just needed to learn. He hadn't gone back to practicing medicine either. He didn't even want to advise me and when I felt sick, he would say: "Best if you consult a doctor." Faced with my astonishment he would assure me that one day he would explain the reason; later on, always later on.

And that "later on" came suddenly, as do so many important things in life that one expects within a certain time and then they turn up when it's not convenient, when one isn't prepared.

Prendel wasn't well. He was nauseated, he'd lost his appetite, he had heat spots. Rather than complaining, he seemed happy. Fifty-two years seemed enough life, he would say. I've already seen what I had to see, he insisted.

Finally his body demanded a solution. And we went to the specialists. He wanted them to be new people, people he wouldn't know from the past. He said he didn't want pity. Or even empathy. What he wanted was a clear diagnosis, nothing more.

When he knew he was sick he decided he had to find a propitious occasion to make me a depository of what he called, with black humour, his legacy. A legacy with which he has been able to live, he said, but one with which he couldn't die.

I needed Prendel to explain his story to me to understand that a shipwreck is a way of disappearing forever, that there is no possible way back. As he had told me more than once, Katy and Frank weren't as dead as him, because they weren't conscious of it, but he was.

He told me during the week we spent in the Boston

Harbor Hotel. He said, "I can't hand over my legacy to you in any old place," and he said it with that characteristic expression of his, the expression that came over his mouth every time he was up to one of his old tricks. I suppose he chose that hotel because from the bedroom we could see the boats sailing on the Charles River. Boats docked at the very entrance to the hotel. Prendel always said that since he'd learned to sail, his world hadn't ended at the seashore or the riverbank. And because of that, from time to time, he would say he also wanted to learn to pilot planes: he didn't want the air to be a limit. "I don't have the credentials to ascend," he would joke.

We hired a boat. Simple and manageable. A twenty-four footer. "A boat for chatting," said Mathew with his customary skill at assigning everything a practical use. In a twenty-four footer you can only be close. And every day of that week, sailing in the *Trevor,* my beloved doctor told me everything I didn't know, all that he'd never told me, everything that I then promised him—and in doing so I remembered my grandfather who always, with every promise, made the same face of disgust as when he tasted something he didn't like and said, "Don't eat that, you'll feel sick,"—I would write on his death.

2.

fter we saw each other again," I remember Dr.
Prendel telling me as we were sailing along and he
was checking that the sails were well-set, "Nelson
Souza, as though he was somehow aware that I wanted to
attack him some time, disappeared. During that second
long absence I devised plans, systems, considered possibilities, but after a time, I began to get disoriented. I don't
know if I'm explaining this very well, Phoebe, I don't
know if I am being faithful to what I really felt back then.
Being disoriented means not knowing anything about anything. For the first time, I wished I'd died. What was I
doing there? What did surviving Frank and Katy mean?"

The days went by as they go by when there is no hope,
like the wind blowing over the land, with no intention. I
stopped recording the passing of time on the rock. If one
doesn't know what is happening, one is not alive, not
aware of being alive. Maybe it was two, maybe four
weeks of not recording. I don't know. Maybe more. The
days, one the same as the next, never pass or pass in a
flash. I'd gone back to scanning the horizon: no ship,
ever. Would I have signaled if I had seen one? How far
does the survival instinct go? Would the fear of Nelson's
threat have outweighed the impulse to try to get them to
see us?

I don't know why we cling to life in such a stubborn way. There are lives not worth living. You will disagree, I know. Our experiences are very different. Your island was Vienna. And your unknown man, your Nelson, was your husband. Your shipwreck, your marriage. You didn't have any reason to take down sails. Or maybe you did? Everyone's own reasons seem the most important. I am not the one to comment on your threshold of endurance.

Our island was not an inhospitable place, not at all. I would even say it received us well. Everything a man needs to survive was there. In fact, a place like that is where one realizes what a man truly needs to survive. And the only essential thing the island couldn't give us was granted by chance: human company. I even understood why Nelson might have saved my life. He wanted a witness to his existence. Someone with whom to be someone. He probably knew that solitude can be equally or even more corrosive than that situation, and it would have sapped his strength. What would I have done? The very same thing: I would have saved the enemy to control him like a dog.

The first phase of not seeing each other had been liberating. The construction of the shelter had kept me busy. I had almost forgotten Nelson's existence, the island, the situation in which I found myself. I mean it, beloved. There came a time when I had the feeling of being exactly where I'd decided to be. Perhaps I hadn't even realized I couldn't escape. I hadn't really noticed, I mean. The awareness of this reality came afterwards, by virtue of the meeting with Souza and his clear, emphatic warnings. I wasn't accustomed to being told what to do. The tension was palpable, you know? That man felt my rebellion, he knew he couldn't lower his guard. And you know what men are in a pure state: savages. Don't look at me with that serious face, Dr. Westore. I know you think we men lack the compassion gene.

We were animals at war. An underground war. Two men alone can be at war, yes, now I am certain. We simply hadn't declared it. But I wanted what he had, and he wanted my obedience: that was enough.

I wanted power, weapons, and above all to control his territory. He'd been able to choose. He must have had some weighty reason to reserve for himself the seeming worst part, don't you think? The narrowest part, with no access to the forest or the mountain, flooded twice a day by the tide. He could have left me there, he would have exercised absolute power over my movements, because that was a natural prison. Why would a man act so, if he wasn't mad? This was one of the obsessive thoughts that was boring into my head. Why? Why? It's easy to have obsessive thoughts on an island, Dr. Westore. Distractions are few and the days are identical to one another, to the point that one feels they are not passing, that time is a mirage, nothing more, and that you have stayed still, as if in a photograph, forever.

Things as they were, however, couldn't go on forever. You know very well that inertia sooner or later will find an obstacle.

Nelson and I went on living our routine. I didn't invade his space, from fear of death, and he didn't let himself be seen, maybe because he thought I was going to ambush him. But, my dear Phoebe, my head never stopped spinning and although I didn't especially want to go back to New York, I became obsessed with the idea of getting out of there.

But let's break this down. Despite the fact that Nelson disappearing again was at first a relief, after a time that as I've already said, I didn't even bother to calculate, I began to feel worried. What if he'd left the island and I hadn't noticed? What if I'd been left alone?

When the tide was low I walked over to his area. From the border I shouted his name a number of times. I knew I was risking my life if I entered his territory without his consent. Nelson didn't answer. Up to a point, it was natural that he didn't hear me, but my unease grew. I decided to respect the pact and not trespass on his land. I couldn't forget that he was armed and, whatever way you look at it, he was a criminal, a pirate, certainly without scruples.

I left my T-shirt tied to a branch near our border. It stood out. Nelson would see it and understand that it was some sort of message. He would come near. Beside the T-shirt, I wrote on the trunk, with a rock, the word "help." I waited nearby until dusk, in case he appeared. He didn't. And I returned to my shelter. That day I had hardly eaten anything except some seaweed. I was hungry and thirsty. When I arrived home, I prepared a little of the fish I had dried days before and I drank a brew of herbs I used as tea.

I spent my nights close to the fire to take advantage of the light, carving chess pieces out of wood I had stripped with the knife. I was working out how long it would take me to finish them and wondered if by the time they were done we would still be there. I was making them to play by myself and with Nelson, if the opportunity arose. For something to do, as well. Just as a God bored of his empty islands had had to carve Nelson and me, for something to do. That was the only time I was on the verge of believing in God. A God as sleepless as I was. Insomnia has always pursued me, as you know. Invariably, every night. Sometimes I gazed up at the stars, I observed with admiration the figures the clouds formed in the black sky or the channels the moonlight sketched on the surface of the sea. I told myself stories, tales, conversations, memories, but it got to the point at which contemplation was killing me, Phoebe, because I identified it with a manner, the most anguished manner, of waiting. And I did count sheep or grains of sand, but it didn't work. Then the idea of chess came to me. To play. Play in that situation? Absolutely. You know my taste for games of any sort, above all those in which intellect plays a special part, and although it may seem strange, in those circumstances this interest didn't abandon me. I had even discovered a plant from which to extract a red dye, to paint and thus distinguish one piece from another. With this same dye I had drawn faces on a rock, I'd written my name and I'd even written down, so they might accompany me, or who knows why, an Auden verse:

What all schoolchildren learn,
Those to whom evil is done
Do evil in return.

I suppose in some way, I was fantasizing about revenge. Fantasies were the only thing I could allow myself.

My signals worked. So the next day, at first light, Nelson was waiting for me at the door of my shelter. As soon as I stuck my head out I heard his voice.

"What do you want? What's wrong? Why are you asking for help?" he asked me, almost without breathing.

"I thought maybe you had left," I said. Why should I lie to him? I saw he was wearing binoculars around his neck. Then it was as if he was watching me. What else did he have that I didn't know about? "Binoculars," I said as I pointed to them.

"Yes. So?"

"I just wanted to know if you were still here. And that you hadn't died. We could take turns visiting," I proposed. "I don't know, once a week, for example."

"I don't think that's necessary," he said.

"One of us could get injured or need help." It seemed reasonable to me to agree on a certain routine. I don't know why I was afraid that Nelson might deceive me. "You have binoculars," I insisted. "You can see me from a distance. I'm not in the same position."

"Of course you're not. So what?"

He started moving away towards his territory.

"Wait, man, wait. It's just you and I, here. I mean we could talk a little. I'll end up going mad, if we don't."

"We'll end up going mad anyway," he assured me. "Losing your mind is part of this experience."

"I want to see your territory," I said straight out. "I think I have a right, and I'm curious to see the other side of the mountain."

"I think you haven't understood anything at all, doctor." Nelson was chewing something and he spat it out. "You say you have a right?"

"This situation isn't fair."

"I saved your life. Full stop. If I hadn't saved you, you wouldn't be here bothering me now." He took off his cap and wiped the sweat with the back of his hand. "This remains as a border. You'll continue to respect it. It hasn't even been four months."

Four months? We'd been on the island that long? However long it was, it had passed almost quickly. There, as I've said, Dr. Westore, time was made of a different material. It really gave the sensation of being fixed, like space, and we moved around inside it as though we were walking through it.

"You mean you'd just as soon we didn't even communicate?"

"Exactly," he said. "When it is time for us to leave, I will tell you. But don't worry." He started walking along the strip of sand, which was beginning to flood. And he added, just before disappearing, "It will be years."

At that point I collapsed, doctor. I became truly conscious of my situation.

"Years?" I was aware that I was shouting. "Years?" I repeated. "What do you mean, years?" I was petrified.

He came back. He grabbed a branch of a nearby tree, as if he might strangle it. And then he said: "Let's see if we understand each other. Although I say you can leave tomorrow, I don't know how you would do it. In the first place, you know as well as I do that there isn't enough wood to build a boat nor the tools necessary to make one more or less reliable. Secondly, the only way to make the pirates believe I'm dead is to die. That is to say, to disappear for as long as possible. I saved your life, don't make me regret it. Technically, you're dead. Got it?"

"Listen, Nelson, we could try building something with the trunk of a fallen tree: there are lots of them and some merchant ship could pick us up miles from here if we head east."

Nelson shook his head from side to side.

"You don't understand. These people aren't like us. If

they hear that a couple of shipwrecks have been rescued and they will hear, believe me, they'll find me."

"Do they have some motive for wanting to annihilate you?"

"The simple fact of having escaped. I know their contacts, their routes, the names of the big fish."

To be honest with you, dear Phoebe, I had the feeling Nelson was exaggerating, like I was watching a film. I was about to ask him another question when he said: "I was preparing for some time to escape from the *Solimán*. I came to it involuntarily. I'm from Lisbon. I've always liked traveling. Five years ago I went to Saint Helena to see where Napoleon was buried. It had always seemed strange that an island would become a prison . . . it doesn't surprise me anymore.

It was clear by this stage that this man and I had things in common. He sat on the ground and went on, while I sat opposite him.

"There I met Cecilia, a beautiful waitress who worked at a bar in the port. I fell in love with her as I never had before and I decided to stay. You know how the threads of life are, you understand them only when they're already wrapped around you.

I thought it was a good sign that Nelson was capable of doing something for love. I don't know why, people capable of falling in love awaken my trust. It's the opposite of what happens to me with people who can't get drunk.

Nelson was ready to tell me his past right up to the end. It's something common in sailors, it's hard for them to talk, but the day they do, it's as if they have made a decision and they act accordingly.

"Cecilia had a brother. In Saint Helena there are few

young men. As soon as they become adults, they escape from a place with no future and less work every day. They needed seamen on the *Solimán.* Through Cecilia's brother, who was a member of the crew and recommended me, they offered me a job. I needed it. I've always made my living from jobs that have come to me. I've been a sailor, a longshoreman, a dog walker, a mechanic . . . but, of course, nobody told me what kind of boat it was. Neither did Cecilia. I don't know if she knew; we never discussed the subject. When I understood, it was already too late, I was in up to my neck."

How often this happens in life, right, Dr. Westore? When you understand, it's already too late. There's no turning back.

"First, I let myself be dazzled by the easy money, I admit that, but soon I realized I was going towards disaster. Five years of renouncing my life, my way of understanding it, my dreams, everything. Five years being a beast at the orders of other beasts."

"Why did you put up with it for so long?" I wanted to know.

How many people live in a skin they don't feel to be their own, right, doctor? It's a great mystery, how we don't dare act according to our desires or convictions and prefer those of others.

"It didn't take long for me to be thinking of a way to escape, but they are mafia, I assure you. I was waiting a long time for the moment to do it. Death seemed the only way to escape. Your shot was my salvation. I'd been ready for so long! And suddenly an impulse, a flash, the moment, I don't know. I almost didn't think. Your shot and the water. I knew of the existence of the island. The old cook on the *Solimán,* Gerardo, the only friend I had among them, certainly because he was also from Lisbon and we could speak in our language without anyone understanding, had spoken to me of this place. I didn't think. I preferred to die rather than continue that life."

Was I supposed to believe him, Phoebe? Did it matter, the truth?

"And Cecilia?" I asked.

"What about Cecilia? Cecilia nothing. She too has to think I'm dead. If one day we get out of here, of course I won't go back to look for her. First and foremost, Cecilia is her brother's sister. Haven't you heard of the bonds instilled by blood?"

My father came into my head. I nodded. I felt overwhelmed. Years! Years on this island? Goaded perhaps by distress, perhaps by Souza's confession, I told him part of my history. Baltimore, New York, Mary, my mother's death, the expectation of my father's death in Texas. My always insatiable desire to sail, the sabbatical year, the preparations for the journey on which I'd lost everything, including my only friends. Souza listened to me, interested, without interrupting, while he drew and wiped away lines in the sand with a stick.

He saw me lose heart, I suppose. And maybe because of that, or who knows why, he gave in.

"Alright, I'll wait for you every Tuesday, in the afternoon. I'll come to read beside this tree."

Understanding that he expected to spend years on that island had disturbed me, but him saying that he would wait for me while reading finished me. Reading? Reading what? He had books? What else did he have?

"Reading?" I asked. "Reading what?"

"I have a couple of books," he said. "I like to read."

"Lots of us sailors like to read," I said. "And write," I added. "Do you have pencil and paper as well?"

He didn't answer, as if I'd violated his privacy.

"Would you be able to lend me one of your books? A little paper?"

"I'll wait at the border, every Tuesday. In the afternoon."

After uttering these words as he might have thrown a stone, he began to move away.

It was clear to me, at that precise instant, that I would invade his territory, dear Phoebe. I would become an invader. And, if I could, I'd rob his loot, whatever it was. And that would amount to a declaration of war, because there'd be no doubt about who had taken it.

Suddenly, I wanted all his belongings. The binoculars, for example. He could see if any ships passed, although they might be distant. He could monitor the frequency of their passing, their flags, the chances of getting their attention. And I wanted the books. He must have things I couldn't even suspect. If the *Solimán's* cook had landed on the island, perhaps he'd left some useful objects.

From that day on, my only thought was to find a way to evade his surveillance. I didn't want to confront him. I wanted to see his shelter when he wasn't there or when he was sleeping. I had to come up with a strategy. Surprise him. Outwit him.

However, we should never underestimate an enemy. Confrontation is like a game of chess: while you are scheming, your opponent is too. The point is seeing which of the rivals is able to think of the biggest number of moves and guess the other's plans.

Tuesday after Tuesday we kept our appointment, checked that we were still alive, both still on the island, and separated again, almost without saying anything. And Tuesday after Tuesday, on seeing him, I would think that I had to come up with some plan. I figured that the best time to attack his territory was on a Tuesday. Swimming in the other direction, far from the place where he waited for me. As a general rule, he arrived first. And there I would see him, sitting near his apron of sand, on a small mound. Binoculars hanging around his neck and, in effect, a book which he left on a rock before approaching me when he saw me appear. There was a lot at stake. I could only attack him once, that was clear. From that moment, it would be war. He would search for me to kill me. Was it worth it, for a book? For the curiosity of seeing what things he had and was hiding from me? Perhaps I could even steal a weapon—at this stage I'd already seen he had more than one. It was unlikely.

On the fifth or sixth Tuesday, I figure towards the end of November, I told him I would trade my watch for his book. Not the knife, I needed my knife and he already had one. No way: he wouldn't agree to any kind of barter.

"What are you reading?"

"A book in Portuguese."

I'd believed he was from Lisbon only because he'd told me so, but in fact he didn't have a foreign accent at all. An armed man is very convincing; or maybe there was just no point in questioning what he said. When all is said and done, Phoebe, the only lies that matter are those that have the power of transforming life, don't you think?

"What book?"

"Are you familiar with Portuguese literature?" His tone was arrogant. Superior.

"Not particularly."

"Then me talking to you about the author of the book is pointless."

"And the other book, is that Portuguese as well?"

"No."

"English, then?"

"Yes, English. Conrad."

"Which? I've read them all."

"Well then one of the ones you've read. I don't know the title. The cover is missing."

"Tell me what it's about. I'll know which one it is."

He began to speak and I recognized the plot of *The Secret Agent*, one of my favorites. The story of two men helping one another. Remember, doctor? We read it together a while ago.

"And you can't lend it to me?"

"I can lend it to you for a week, if you catch me twelve good fishes."

"Twelve? That's madness. You know how hard it is to catch them."

"Do you want the book?"

Of course I wanted it, Phoebe. I'd never wanted a book as much as I did then. I would be able to do something that animals couldn't do, I'd feel like a man and not a beast. I remembered the typical question, what book would you take to a desert island? Now my answer would be—any book at all. Whichever, Dr. Westore. Even the book in Portuguese, written in a language I don't understand in the least, would have kept me company.

"All right. In two weeks I'll bring the fish. Next week don't expect me."

Why did he want to get out of working? For what did

Nelson Souza want time? Fishing was perhaps one of the most entertaining activities, one of the things that made you feel better, at least it did me.

He seemed upset. Perhaps these encounters had become a comfortable way for him to check up on me.

"A dozen will be worth a week's loan," he said before leaving. "It's the rainy season," he warned. "Try to find a better place than the one you have."

I was grateful for the information. Days before I'd found an almost invisible inlet between some rocks. A type of cave I'd only approached by night, when Nelson couldn't see me. I'd sought it when faced with the threat of heavy rain, yes, but also in case one day I needed to hide from him. Some nights I slept there. But I emerged before the first rays of sunlight, in case he was watching me.

I brought him the dozen fish he'd requested. Nelson had a net to collect them. A net he couldn't have sewn with the materials on the island. A net, therefore, that was already there, one of his belongings I didn't know about. A great tool. I pretended not to notice it. Of course, he also had the book for me. It wasn't only the cover that was missing. Some pages at the beginning were missing. The already short novel was now scarcely a few pages. When he handed it to me, I immediately put it under my T-shirt, as if it were the greatest of treasures.

"I want it here next Tuesday."

"We'll be here." I spoke in the plural about the book and myself. A telling plural, I thought. If there'd been a mammal on the island, I surely would have made it into a pet. I needed to talk and not only talk. There were days when I felt I was on the verge of going mad, when I doubted my existence, or more than doubted, I became aware of its insignificance. Living for the sake of living, living so as not to die. Nobody, except Nelson, knew I was alive; it was like not living. In some moments I wished I were dead. Not to die, no. To be dead, yes, to have done it. And on the contrary, I was incapable of killing another or killing myself. Hippocratic oath? *I will not give a lethal drug to anyone if I am asked, nor will I advise such a plan.*

But the following Tuesday we didn't go back. Or the next. I went four weeks without showing up at the appointment, hidden every Tuesday in my secret, or what I considered secret, cave. I imagined Nelson waiting for me. I imagined him becoming furious, evaluating the possibility of coming in search of what belonged to him, hating me, shouting at me, watching with his binoculars in vain. I also thought, other days, that he would appear at any moment and without any ado he would kill me. I had trouble sleeping and I lived in a constant state of alert. My defiance was puerile, I know, but in those circumstances, my darling, in those circumstances the brain doesn't function normally. One's values, priorities, and emotions get disrupted. One clutches at straws. For me the book became a bridge, a kind of visa, a symbol of return. It was my victory.

In fact, my attitude was not the same as before. I went back to marking time, trying to stay clean, hiding to do my bodily needs and burying them, reclaiming part of the civilization from whence I came. With an inexact calculation, I even had a kind of solitary New Year's Eve celebration. I was feeling strong and optimistic.

On the fifth Tuesday I went alone, without Conrad. I'd decided to tell him a lie. I'd decided to tell him I'd lost it. However far-fetched my argument seemed, it was my word against his. Against his word and his weapons, yes, but was he going to kill me over a book? I weighed up the risk. It was impossible to kill a man over a book.

But it wasn't about a book. It was about the order of things. Discipline. Power. You know the value of symbols, my darling.

When Dr. Prendel returns to the border after having missed four Tuesdays, Souza isn't there. Nor any trace of him. The silence seems terrifying. He realizes that he has assessed his situation badly. He regrets not having come to the previous appointments. He regrets being there without the book. He fears for his life.

He calls Souza. Until dusk. Even after night has fallen. Nothing. Nothing at all. He will have to wait until the following Tuesday.

Three weeks go by. Souza has given no signs of life, he hasn't appeared on any Tuesday. Or any day, in fact. Mathew knows this because, obsessed by the possible repercussions, he has gone every afternoon. He has spent hours with the book in his hands, waiting for Souza's appearance. He has left the T-shirt on the branch again. He has even left the book wrapped in the T-shirt. Nothing. Nothing at all.

Dr. Prendel asks himself if Souza is still alive. He thinks he has to respect his absence. A bitter struggle is unfolding between his desire, curiosity, and common feeling. What if he is injured? What if he has died? Worse: what if he has left? The same uncertainty must have tortured Souza during his disappearance. And despite having a compelling reason, recovering his book, Nelson Souza has not come looking for him. He has proudly shown that he doesn't depend on Mathew at all, shown him his indifference. It is as though he had said: you are the one who asked for the appointments; I don't need to see you; sooner or later you'll come, you'll give me back the book and ask my forgiveness. Nelson is punishing him.

The days are all the same. One after another like links in an absurd, rusty chain that leads nowhere. An endless chain.

Prendel can't stand the pressure any longer. He doesn't have a grand plan, but neither does he have the patience necessary to find one. Prendel is a man of action and he doesn't know that life goes on even when it isn't pushed.

He decides to break the pact. He will go over to the other side. He'll do it at night, definitely. He waits for a full moon.

And when the night he is waiting for comes, he doesn't hesitate. He is carrying one of the syringes of anesthetic from the first-aid kit and keeps four more vials in his pocket. There is enough to defend himself, to put him to sleep and, if necessary, to kill him.

He leaves his shelter and walks with confidence and precision. When he gets to the vicinity of the forbidden zone, he will crawl. He will try not to make noise.

He lies down on the sand, which is damp. He smells it and remembers his arrival on the island, which seems distant now. It is not long since the tide went out. He advances skirting the mountain, hardly able to see anything. The brightness of the moon isn't enough. He scans the darkness, eyes wide open. His breathing seems loud. His heart is beating with an unknown rapidity. Calm down, Mathew, calm down, he tells himself silently. Nelson must be sleeping, he says, he surely isn't lying in wait now, he repeats. He takes a deep breath. He presses his eyelids with his thumb and index finger. He wants to calm himself. For a moment, he considers the possibility of turning back. He moves forward when he feels his heart beating at a more normal rate. As soon as he begins to move, however, it races once again. He keeps going.

It doesn't take him long to cover the distance separating him from the other side. He feels nerves throughout his body. He calls it nerves, but he could just as well call it fear. He advances, crouching. He takes only three steps. On the third, a shot causes him to stiffen. First he thinks it has passed very close to him. He has heard its whistle. But immediately he discovers that it has lodged in his thigh, almost in the groin. It's bleeding. It burns his flesh. He plugs the injury with a hand. The bullet is inside, the muscle tissue destroyed. He thanks his lucky stars that it hasn't hit his femoral artery. He falls to the ground. He doesn't dare move, forwards or backwards. He hears noises. Souza is approaching. He is carrying a lantern. It shines in his eyes and blinds him.

"I was expecting you. It's taken you a while." He tuts. "Did you think I wouldn't be alert with the tide out?"

"I'm wounded." Prendel is dizzy.

"I should have killed you."

"We're even."

"Don't try it again, doctor, don't do it. Next time the bullet will go straight to your head."

Prendel looks up and struggles to make out the figure of Souza. He searches underneath his T-shirt. He gives him the book. He stains it with blood. Souza grabs it abruptly. Protected by the darkness, Prendel takes advantage of the moment to get rid of the syringe and vials. The risk of keeping them and Souza discovering them was too great. The other man helps him to get up and ties his hands behind his back.

"I don't think there's any need . . . " Prendel tries to complain, but Souza pretends not to hear him. The doctor lets him do it, he doesn't dare fight against an armed man, and so much the less, wounded as he is. Souza carries Prendel. They move through the darkness. Nelson pants. Both are well-built; he finds it difficult to drag Prendel, who can barely walk.

When they get to Souza's shelter, Mathew is speechless. They are in a wide area deep inside the mountain. There is a fire lit which generously illuminates the whole space. Mathew glances around rapidly. Nelson Souza lives a life very different to him. Nelson has canned foods, glasses and cutlery, whisky and cigarettes, saucepans to heat food, and worst and most serious of all, he has a lifeboat. Now he understands where he got the medical kit, the fishing tackle, and now he realizes that he must have a full kit of flares and signals to make their presence on this damned island known. Mathew understands why Nelson has wanted to veto Mathew's access to his territory from the beginning. He didn't want him to see the boat, be able to get to it. Nelson has his safe passage prepared and didn't want Prendel to know. He'd certainly figured that the doctor wouldn't tolerate spending an indefinite amount of time on the island if he discovered the existence of a means of leaving.

Souza also ties up his legs. Mathew has become a prisoner of war. All the while they have not exchanged a single word. Finally, Prendel passes out.

When he wakes again it is day. He is still tied up. He is lying on a bed of leaves. Beside him he sees the medical kit he had been keeping in his hut. Nelson is nearby, he calls him.

"You've been unconscious," Souza explains. "I took the opportunity to go looking for the medical kit in your cabin," he says sarcastically. "I've injected you with morphine, I've removed the bullet and I've stitched up the injury as well as I could. Gerardo taught me one day, with some dead rabbits. We sewed up a few. I've done it in the same way."

"You having experience is a comfort," says Prendel ironically, confirming at the same time that Nelson knows the rudiments of basic medicine and is a self-sufficient man.

"By the way, I saw that there were four vials of anesthetic missing and by chance I found them along the way, near where I shot you."

Prendel knows it's an accusation. He doesn't answer, he doesn't protest.

Souza tells him he will spend a few days there, with him, until he is well enough to leave again.

"Why haven't you left me to die?" Prendel wants to know. "Now I owe you two lives."

Souza smiles.

"I'm not a killer," says Souza. "There are places it's impossible to come back from," he assures him. "I've seen truly disturbed people, after committing a crime, doctor. People lose their minds. I don't recommend it."

"Man, I save . . . used to save lives."

"Used to save, of course. Here you almost put an end to one, mine."

"In self-defense."

Souza shrugs. The doctor continues: "The truth is that it had already been a while since I practiced medicine before going traveling. I used to teach at the university but I didn't feel comfortable there either."

And Prendel explains some of the reasons he decided to make the journey in the *Queen* to Nelson Souza. And what he felt when he found himself alone in the middle of the Atlantic, watching how his friends stayed behind, how his boat was moving away. His salvation and his past, all together, all at once. Life.

"You didn't have a bad life in New York. I've always wanted to go," declares Souza. "I think I'd have liked to have been born there, on the other side of the Atlantic.'

"You won't find anything you don't have anywhere else," Prendel comments and with a gesture asks for a cigarette, which Souza passes him already lit.

"Well people always dream of what they haven't got. Maybe you would like to have been born in Europe or what do I know, Argentina." Nelson lights a cigarette for himself as well. He inhales the smoke, holds it inside for a moment and then expels it with force, gasping, as if he might also expel wishes that have never become reality.

Dr. Prendel shakes his head.

"What matters is what you do with your life, not where you do it."

Nelson doesn't answer. He seems pensive. Prendel feels tired. He puts out his cigarette, lies down, and falls asleep.

Those days while the doctor is recovering from his injury, he and Souza have long conversations. About family, the past, the future. At first begrudgingly; then with the spirit necessity bestows. It can't be said that they establish a bond of friendship because Prendel's hands and legs are still tied, and Souza is still armed, in a state of alert. It is certain, however, that they arrive at a closeness lent by the conviction that if they emerge from the exceptional situation uniting them, they will probably never see each other again.

After ten days, the doctor begins to move his leg. He has made no attempt to escape, it is obvious that he has nowhere to go. What's more, he is still tied up. Souza fears an attack and only unties him under surveillance, so he can take care of his bodily needs or eat.

"I think I'm well enough to go," Prendel comments one morning when Souza returns from fishing.

"Of course you can assess your condition much better than I can, doctor."

Prendel asks Souza to help him stand up, takes a few steps.

"Tomorrow," he says. "Or the day after."

"No hurry," Souza reassures him.

"Thank you for almost killing me," says Prendel as he sits down again. "And for not doing it," he adds with a bitter smile. "Although look, truth is, maybe you'd have done me a favor. Nothing is waiting for me, on land. I'll live embittered by all that's happened, blaming myself for having led my friends to their deaths, raging about my failure, useless, unable to give classes or operate, maybe living with my father, retired in Georgetown hoping death comes for me before it does for him. As long as I'm here, I feel I'm expiating my guilt. The suffering is useful to me. You, on the other hand, want to live, return to the world, to find once again what you left behind. Do you have family?"

"When I left Lisbon my parents were alive, yes, and I have a brother and sister, Miguel and Lidia. Lidia is two years younger than me, a math teacher in the school where we studied together. Miguel is a motorbike mechanic. He's married and has two children. My parents have a grocery store in the Alfama neighborhood."

Prendel thinks that Nelson is surely inventing everything he tells him, but it doesn't occur to him to reproach him because in the middle of that night of misfortune, he feels in the mood for the most common story in the world, the ABCs of a family and their work and bonds. He wants to hear about these things.

He himself has told a number of lies and some truths, as if he were chatting from his apartment in Manhattan, and he assumes Souza has done the same. He understands that it is not the stories that matter, but the act of telling them to each other. At these moments, they don't need someone familiar, in the profound sense of the word, but a companion, someone at their side who talks, says anything, humanizes them. The next day, Prendel is sure that he is well enough to leave. Eleven days have gone by. Souza has made sure that he's had everything he needed. The island of contradictions, Prendel baptizes it. He's been searching for a name for it for days. He mentions it to Souza, who says:

"Does it seem important to you doctor, what this forsaken piece of land is called?" He raises his index finger to his temple and rotates it to signal that Prendel has got a few scews loose.

"Putting a name on things seems a good way of making them exist," adds Prendel, not too convinced. And he thinks that maybe, without realizing it, they both are going through transitory moments of madness. That asphyxiating heat, that situation, are not for nothing. And in this state, they are capable of anything. At times he thinks that if only they could manage to escape from there, if they could reach civilization together, they could be friends. His hatred is becoming tolerance. What would he have done in Souza's place? To consider the question is to begin to get outside of himself and become able to see the world, for an instant at least, through other eyes. What would he have done? And he realizes he isn't capable of giving himself a single answer.

"Now I know you know I have a boat, Prendel. Now I won't lower my guard. Careful what you do. I guarantee you we will leave here. I told you I had a plan. And I have. But it will be when I say, understood?"

Prendel nods. He has no choice but to obey orders.

"I can't trust you, you made that clear. The book was a test, Prendel. I thought: if he doesn't bring it back to me after a week, he can't be trusted. Pacts, although they might be made about small things, are made to be fulfilled. You have to keep your word. And also, you invaded my territory. If you'd stayed in your zone until I came to look for you . . . "

"Would you have come?'

"No doubt."

"When?"

"Whenever, a month, three months, a year."

Prendel laughs in a stentorian manner.

"A year!"

"Time passes quickly. Life does, Prendel. A year here is nothing. Nothing changes in a year, except how you see someone. In a year, we would have built a solid trust."

"And why do I want your solid trust?"

"To get off the island, for example? To share in the privileges I have at my disposal?"

Souza heats water in a small saucepan, to make coffee.

"And where has all this come from?"

"Why should I tell you?"

"What could I do with your information, apart from eat it?"

Prendel's tone was defiant, in spite of his situation being much worse than Nelson's. "We've been here over half a year," Prendel comments, as if he is speaking to himself, but sure the other man is listening. And he adds in a hostile tone: "Half a year of sacrifices decided by you. Wasn't it enough for you to see me lose my friends, my yacht, my life? How did you expect me not to try to steal a damn book from you?"

Nelson takes the saucepan off the fire. He asks:

"Coffee?"

"Whiskey?" Prendel dares to suggest. Souza agrees and adds a few drops.

"I won't repeat it. It was a test. We are all put to the test, Prendel. Everyone is suspicious of everyone. Proof, proof, we ask for proof for everything. The other man's word isn't enough for us, we need him to prove what he says. That's our tragedy. How do I know I can trust you? How do I know I can take you into the boat when we can finally leave here?"

"You can't." Prendel knew he was risking his life with that declaration. He knew, however, Nelson wouldn't believe him if he said the opposite.

Souza laughs. Prendel smiles.

"How did you know there was a boat on the island?"

"Telling you won't help you."

"To satisfy my curiosity, at least."

"Gerardo, the *Solimán*'s cook left all this here. He felt sorry for me, Gerardo. He confessed the island's existence to me and assured me that, for pertinent circumstances he'd kept enough stuff to survive. He told me so I might try to escape, I suppose. Because he thought I wouldn't succeed, certainly. Or perhaps he thought I'd propose we escape together, I don't know. Old Gerardo, if he's still alive, must think from time to time that maybe I am here. If he said it to the others, however, he would have to admit that he spoke to me about the existence of the island and that revelation would compromise his safety. His hands are tied."

"And how much time has to go by before they will have forgotten about you?"

"Mortality among pirates is high, Prendel. They die, they kill each other, their victims kill them. I'm confident that within a few years some will be caught and others will have snuffed it."

Prendel, determined to return to his cage, begins to walk towards the apron of sand which leads to the other part of the island.

"I'll take advantage of low tide," he says.

Souza stops him: "Wait."

He gives him the binoculars. Another test? wonders Prendel. And after Prendel thanks him and begins walking once again towards his zone, Souza follows him and says:

"I think this is yours now."

He is referring to the Conrad. Prendel takes it. He looks at Souza, guards the book under his T-shirt, pulls down his cap and leaves, limping, little by little.

4.

From that moment on, Prendel lives in desperation. Knowing about the existence of the boat has upset him. Now, indeed, he feels like a prisoner. He can't escape, he can't attack. All he can do is wait, survive and wait.

But now things are clear between them. Souza is seen more often. There are nights he even plays a game of chess, which Prendel always wins.

"You have to obtain a victory in something," Nelson provokes him. "Where I won't tolerate losing is in life," he adds.

And Prendel asks him how he knows if he is winning or losing in life. How does he know, if so often when it seems one is losing, in reality he is winning.

Prendel will keep the chess game forever. It symbolizes the game he won against life, if surviving is winning.

Some storms, calm days, crests of unbearable anxiety and moments of complete neglect.

Prendel can't stop going over the same thing: he doesn't understand why Nelson is postponing the departure. He doesn't believe his explanations. They don't add up. He contemplates the possibility that Nelson is not right in the head, that he has truly lost the ability to perceive. What does he do, day after day, on his minuscule strip of island?

He knows it's risky, that he shouldn't do it, because the Atlantic might betray him, because the sharks aren't far away, because Souza might see him, but Prendel decides to swim, to wade into the sea straddling a tree trunk to help him float and get to the peak of the island where the enemy lives. He wants to see what he is doing. He needs to know more.

So on a relatively calm day, a day when the wind is not blowing too strong and the sea is not too deep, a day with good visibility, Prendel calculates the hour at which the sun won't blind him when he faces the island and goes out determined, with the binoculars around his neck.

Shortly after starting to swim he becomes paralyzed. He is scared of drowning. The days spent in the sea, just after losing his friends and boat, haunt his imagination. His legs stiffen, his breathing is labored, he feels he is about to have a heart attack. He flounders, swallows water, comes up to the surface again, coughs, feels dizzy, the trunk slips away, he can't see anything, he feels something hard brush again his legs, a shark, he shouts, his thigh injury stabs him so painfully it is almost unbearable, he is lost. Prendel thinks Souza is about to be left alone on the island. And this thought, as if it were a needle sticking into a nerve ending, revives him, returns him to the world. Nothing. No interruptions. One stroke after another. He goes out far enough that Nelson, should he see a shape, won't be able to identify him. Nelson doesn't have binoculars. He arrives at the place he has calculated, just opposite Souza's cave. He leans on the trunk again, grabs the binoculars, adjusts them and searches for the man. It doesn't take him long to find him. And it doesn't take him long, either, to realize that he doesn't understand what he is doing. It seems as if Nelson Souza is looking for something. He hits some objects he can't identify with a tool he can't identify either. He moves from side to side. He sits down, waits, goes back. Suddenly he shoots his gun. Prendel hides his face under the water. Has he seen him? When he returns to the surface he discovers that Souza is still shooting, but he is shooting first into the sand, then at the mountain and a moment later into the air. Now Prendel is convinced: Nelson has lost his mind. Sometimes, from his part of the island he had heard shots, but he'd thought Nelson was shooting at a snake, a fish. He watches him a little longer, which only confirms his worst fears. Nelson Souza appears to be a half-wit with a foolish obsession.

Clearly he has been under the yoke of a madman, a man with no capacity for reason, or even worse, an armed man with no capacity for reason. How many times do weapons accompany dementia, or the reverse? Maybe Nelson Souza had lost his mind working for the pirates, while he swam terrified towards the island, conscious that his bleeding injury could attract sharks. Or perhaps it had been on the island. Indeed it was no secret that islanders have a tendency to delirium, and how, then, would he not go mad, a man arriving on the island accidentally, a man who has been forced to stay there.

Prendel begins to swim towards the shore again, supported by the trunk. Night is falling, the little light remaining simply outlines the profile of the mountain, intensifies the color of things; he has the sensation of looking at an Impressionist painting, a painting that can only be appreciated from afar, that loses its meaning up close. Maybe it is he who doesn't know what he is saying. Can he be sure he still has the ability to reason? And in that case, what is he doing swimming in the Atlantic to spy on an armed man who has threatened him with death?

Maybe neither of them is in his right mind. How can they be sure they still have their mental health? What type of test should be done to find out? They don't have visions, they don't hear voices inside their heads, they don't think of themselves as Messiahs. Is that enough?

Prendel arrives at his beach. He is naked. Weary, he lies down on the sand. He remembers when he always used to do the same, as a child, when his parents took him to the beach. His flesh would be covered and his mother would scold him because she used to find sand in the house for days and days afterwards. And for the first time since his arrival on the island, Prendel weeps.

5.

A man with no objective begins to abandon his condition as a man and move closer to that of an animal. Prendel no longer has any purpose. He'd wanted to catch Souza by surprise, he has tried to steal his weapons, he has pleaded, he has begged him. He has waited. He has despaired. He has reasoned. He has been useless. He has fruitlessly tried to build a boat. He has swum kilometers to escape, and he's had to return, beaten.

In the end, he has given up. He has abandoned himself to the island, has become part of it. He has renounced any purpose in life and has reduced himself to surviving the way his prey do, be they worms, lizards or insects. He moves only when strictly necessary. He has completely lost any notion of time and his memory is blocked. He has thrown his watch into the sea, he does not mark the days that pass on the stone calendar. He assumes he will never be able to leave there. He is in no hurry, but he has decided that one day or another he will end up committing suicide.

Prendel spends the days beside his shelter, which is now no more than a ruin under a sunshade. He's had to construct a few since his arrival. They crumble from the rain, the wind, and the sun. He feels that in some way he is the perfect reproduction of his father in the garden of his house in Georgetown. He thinks that if he had to end up like the old man, he loses nothing by bringing it forward a few years. At times he gets up, wets his feet at the sea's edge and returns. Every day he chooses a fixed point on which to keep his gaze. From time to time he sees Souza pass by. They haven't spoken for a while. They don't need to.

Souza has sometimes come over to him, brought him something to eat, told him to have patience, not much longer now. Prendel doesn't listen. He doesn't believe him and doesn't care.

* * *

One day, probably months later, Nelson Souza comes running over to him, exultant.

"We can go. In two or three days we can go, Prendel. We only have to get things ready and we can go."

Prendel doesn't answer, or even look at him. Maybe he doesn't believe him, maybe he doesn't hear him.

"Prendel!" Souza shouts, comes close, shakes him. He is excited. We can go. And you know why? Because I've found what I was looking for. You hear? I've found what I was looking for. So we can go."

These are the words Prendel needed as a hook to grab onto and return to reality. Hope always needs a point of departure. He has found what he was looking for? Is that what he said? In other words, he was looking for something, it wasn't his imagination, Souza was mad but there was a method to his madness.

"We have to gather enough water and food. It'll be many miles before we find some ship that can rescue us, you hear?" Souza doesn't seem the same, he talks fast, in a very firm voice. He's beside himself. He truly seems like another man.

What can he have found? Prendel doesn't dare ask for an explanation. What does it matter, if they're going to leave at last. Little by little his brain begins to stir. He notes that at the moment the wind is blowing from the south-west, the wind most favorable to their leaving the island in the lifeboat. The current will help them get away. His heart races. Maybe, he thinks. Yes, maybe. The man living within him reacts.

He finally gets up, looks at Souza. How can he be sure that man isn't going to kill him as soon as they get into the boat, or even before, or after they're spent days at sea and begin to run short of water and food. But each of them needs the other. Better two than one for rowing. Better two than one for everything. Souza had said very clearly that there no reason to kill a man who might be useful. They need to trust one another. It's not that they trust each other, it's that they need to.

They divide the work. Prendel will see to the water. He will have to fill all the containers he can find, in addition to the canteens. Souza is in charge of the food. Once they leave the island they can't go back. They have to be sure they are taking all the necessary steps.

They are three frenetic days. They go through what they will need again and again. They're anxious. They're euphoric. They're about to leave.

The night before departure they drink what whisky they have left. They relax. They are in Souza's hut, in his territory. They know that soon they are going to share a much smaller and dangerous space than an island. Some difficult days.

"I don't owe you an explanation," says Souza, but I'm going to give you one."

Prendel waits. There is a full moon. The fire they used to cook dinner is now only embers. Souza had kept some cigarettes. They smoke. There is a kind of normality in what they are doing, as if they have come back to civilization.

"I told you that I'd found what I was looking for."

Prendel shrugs his shoulders and confesses, down to the last detail, his excursion with the binoculars, the way in which he'd spied on Souza and discovered that he was looking for something. He has nothing to lose now.

Souza gives no importance to the revelation, as if he already knew what had happened. He explains that he'd been on the verge of going mad, he'd come to think that what he was seeking didn't exist, that it had all been a practical joke of Gerardo's, or the product of delirium.

Prendel listens, expectant.

"This was what I was looking for," says Nelson Souza, and shows Prendel three small dark bags. "Diamonds."

Then he tells him that the *Solimán* runs the guns that feed African wars and gets paid in diamonds. A while before, Gerardo had convinced his assistant, a naive young boy, that they should make the most of a chance to keep some of the loot. Gerardo had a plan. They'd moored in a port for a few days.

"They were in Nigeria, in the harbor at Lagos. They were supposed to stay there a couple of weeks. They were waiting for a new shipment of weapons. The diamonds from the last delivery were aboard. Gerardo knew where. He persuaded the assistant that they could steal a yacht to reach the island. Once there, they would hide the diamonds and return aboard without anyone knowing. After a time, when everything calmed down, they would go back for them. Everything went to plan. But as to be expected, Gerardo hadn't explained the whole plan to the young man. Once they got to the island and hid the loot, Gerardo killed the assistant, lowered the lifeboat, and returned alone to leave the yacht where he'd found it. With luck, nobody would have missed it. The pleasure yachts spend months sleeping in the ports with nobody visiting them. And anyway, he had invented a culprit. Nobody on the *Solimán* would doubt that the assistant had stolen the stones and escaped without a trace."

Prendel looks at Nelson with horror and says: "So easy. A clean job, indeed."

"Life is hard, doctor. And when one sees he is approaching the end, sometimes he takes drastic measures." Nelson takes a gulp from his cup of whisky. He finishes it and pours himself more.

Prendel follows his example and asks Souza to finish telling him the story. He figures Souza has lowered his guard, he knows that he is no longer a threat, that the only thing he wants is to leave the island and now that he has admitted it, he has nothing to fear now.

"Gerardo thought about returning to the island one way or another. Precisely because he didn't know how or with whom, he'd left a full survival kit. A little before the attack on the *Queen,* the old cook had come down with a fever. Malaria. At times he was delirious. The doctor said he wasn't going to make it."

Souza told the story to the end. Prendel listened to him as if, in fact, he was narrating a fictional adventure.

When the *Solimán* attacked Dr. Prendel's boat, Gerardo, plagued by the threat of death, had already told the whole story to Souza. He didn't tell him, however, where he'd hidden the loot, maybe because he thought keeping the secret was the only way of making sure Souza would try to keep him alive.

Souza had decided that he wouldn't leave the island without the diamonds. It was a matter of a real fortune. Enough for numerous men to live numerous lives of real luxury.

"To compensate you, I'll give you some." And he throws him one of the bags.

Prendel can't believe it; he's speechless. Souza could have taken much longer to find the diamonds, years perhaps. It could have been a cook's delirium. Others could have found them before Souza got to the island. They could have spent the rest of their lives there alone because this man had the stupid ambition of making himself rich. He is furious and explodes. He screams at him, insults him, feels deceived, cheated, mocked. He throws the bag of diamonds in Souza's face.

"You seriously think a fistful of diamonds is important enough to hold someone prisoner?"

"It's what makes the world go round, let's not kid ourselves."

"Other things make the world go round. You wanted to escape the pirates because you think you're different. Don't deceive yourself, you're even worse."

Souza stands up. Prendel had done so a moment before. The men's silhouettes stand out against the darkness, illuminated by the firelight. Nelson adjusts the two weapons at his disposal on his belt. Prendel takes a step back. He assesses his situation: he cannot confront Nelson just now. He keeps quiet.

"You're making a mistake," Souza says to him. "You'll see you're making a mistake." He stretches, yawns, rubs his face with both hands. "We should rest a little."

At that moment, Prendel realizes it is very likely that Nelson may try to kill him before daybreak. If not, why has he told him the story, and, even worse, been ready to share his fortune with him? Prendel knows that diagnoses are made based on symptoms and there is no doubt that these are very clear.

Dr. Prendel is a victim of terror. He doesn't want to leave Nelson alone, because he is afraid he will set sail without him, but neither does he want to stay at his side, because he's afraid of going to sleep and never waking up again.

The two men move a few meters apart. Both are thin, bearded, bare chested. They look alike. Each one prepares his place to spend the night. Prendel stays seated with his back against a rock. He smokes a last cigarette. He knows he should sleep, that he needs to rest because, in the best of cases, days of hard, exhausting sailing await him, in the company of a stranger who he cannot or doesn't want to trust, but he can't close his eyes. And it is strange that he can't, because if he has learned anything from sailing alone it is how to fall asleep quickly, anywhere, and for short bursts.

He looks at the other man, still awake, and it all seems monstrously natural. Perhaps it was the whisky, which has made them a little too relaxed.

He raises his head and recognizes the stars. Betelgeuse, Rigel, Bellatrix. Sirius, Aldebaran. The seven sisters. And Castor and Pollux. He has always liked the names of the stars. And by guiding himself more by the stars than the compass. Despite having to change the guiding star every so often, as the situation developed and changed. I will not see them from this island any more, he thinks without nostalgia. In a few days all this will all be over and he will be another man.

6.

And this is the point I wanted to get to, Phoebe," Dr. Prendel confessed while we were moving with a tailwind towards the port. "You will forgive my circling around it for so long. You probably think I am a monster. But you must understand me. You must understand me. Only you can. I know I should have killed myself the following day, Dr. Westore. I wasn't capable of trusting that man. I betrayed all of my principles. I wasn't capable of respecting human life. And I'm not going to deny it: it wasn't only fear that I felt; the diamonds also clouded my mind. I figured that, like me, the other man would try to spend the night awake. By the early morning however, I saw that sleep had overtaken him and he was sleeping deeply. I don't remember if I had a moment's doubt or if the impulse won me immediately. I rose and, little by little, I moved closer to him. Once at his side, I grabbed a weapon with a quick violent movement and I shot him once, decisively. I shot him again, and this time I think he died. He went to sleep with the idea that the next day we would set sail and we would be equal, both of us impossible survivors. I am equally tortured by the idea of having killed him as that of having left him badly injured. Can you imagine?

Moments after the shooting I was already in the

lifeboat, rowing out to sea, with my heart thumping from the two things I'd just done: killed a man and saved myself.

Would you be able to forgive me? I have tried all these years in vain.

It wasn't until many miles later I found his letter. To be precise, his letters. One in English, addressed to me. Another in Portuguese, for his family in Lisbon. The one for his family I am giving to you now, Dr. Westore, so you can get it there. It took me a while to read it; I did so when I met someone who could translate it for me. Everything he'd told me was true. His adventurous spirit, his parents' grocery store, his siblings, his love for Cecilia, that sort of kidnapping the pirates had subjected him to, and his desire to escape, the cook's information. Souza wasn't lying. He was an honest man. Any lie of his would perhaps have made my betrayal more bearable. It is important that you get in contact with his family. Although it may be late, they have to know that their son, their brother is dead. It is a debt I owe them, do you understand?

I destroyed the letter addressed to me. I threw it into the sea instantly, as though it might burn my fingers. He said I would only have found the letter if I had killed him. And if I had killed him, he asked me to make sure the other missive got to his family and he felt sorry for me, because I would never find a way of leaving that island.

And so it was, Dr. Westore. I am still there, trying every day, to take back what I did. How irreparable is death and how different a man is after killing. How well have I seen it. I am happy that the end is coming for me, dear Phoebe, because it will be the only way of ending the guilt.

You must excuse me for not having told you before. But of what would a man like me not be capable? I have despised myself all the days of my life since I climbed into the boat. I've wanted to convince myself that the other man would have killed me on the way, that he would not have been capable of sharing the diamonds with me and even less the scarce food and water for so many days as we might have needed before finding salvation. In vain. He was a real man. He would not have killed me, but I killed him to prevent him from doing so.

The diamonds. Most of them are still in my possession. He was right. There are enough of them for many men to live many lives. They are for you.

I have lived all these years with this secret, but I cannot die with it. Publish my story with names and surnames, Dr. Westore. And know that if I ask you this, it is so as to die peacefully, no more. I am a wretch and I think that perhaps this confession will serve in part to expiate my guilt."

EPILOGUE

I stayed with Dr. Prendel until he died without questioning what opinion someone capable of killing like that, in cold blood, deserved from me. My grandfather would have said: "You can't trust a man who sails alone. Would you trust an animal who isolates itself from the herd?"

Afterwards I requested a leave of absence to go to Lisbon. It wasn't part of the promise, but the letter of the doctor's victim troubled me and I needed to meet the Souzas. I wasn't doing it for Prendel, I was doing it for myself. Perhaps to understand why a man is capable of doing what the doctor had done, how a person is capable of transforming themselves to this extreme.

Now that I am here, I have finished writing what Mathew told me, and I am about to meet Nelson's family, my strength falters. Do I have to tell them that their son is dead? Should I give them an old, faraway letter, written by someone who has not existed for so long? I'm so filled with doubt that I leave the hotel, take a taxi, and give the address, still not knowing what I am going to say. I am carrying, indeed, the letter in my bag, as if my bag were the bottle a hopeful shipwreck throws into the sea. I have read it more than once: "Dear parents and siblings, if this letter reaches your hands, whenever it may come and whoever brings it to you, he will want to say that a short time ago I died . . . " Poor Nelson, he thought that a man capable of killing him would have the decency to act as messenger.

It wasn't too difficult to locate the Souzas. The directions Nelson had given Mathew were enough. The family agreed to receive me because, when I contacted them by telephone from New York, I told them I had news of their missing son and I preferred to give it to them in person. Luckily, I had studied Portuguese in university and although it was rusty, I could manage.

I arrive at the Souzas' house. A woman of approximately my age who must be Lidia, Nelson's sister, opens the door to me. And yes, she is Lidia, because she tells me so right away, as she leads the way to the sitting room. A small room, full of furniture covered in shiny, imitation-wood Formica. It is midday, but as it is hot, they have the blind half-lowered so there is a kind of semi-darkness. They ask me to sit down at the table, covered with an oil-cloth stamped with drawings of coffee pots, cups, cutlery, and all sorts of kitchen utensils. I lean on it and my sweaty arms stick to the plastic. When I raise them, embarrassed, it rises a little. They serve me a glass of red wine and some cheese tacos. They sit around me, except Miguel, the brother, who remains standing. The mother watches me anxiously. She doesn't dare ask. Her son has been dead for years, she thinks. She hasn't heard anything about him for almost twenty years. They have tried everything. They've always failed. The earth has swallowed him up. Or the sea.

"Nelson was an adventurer," says the father, and he speaks in the past tense. He has discovered in my expression that his suspicions are not unfounded. "Nelson wasn't like his siblings; he needed to fly." And he breathes deeply, as if in place of air he seeks comfort. "He went to Saint

Helena; he called it the prison island. And you see it was a prison, he never came back. He had a girlfriend there. She never heard from him again either. His shipmates told her he was lost at sea during a storm."

I understand that when he speaks of Nelson's ship-mates he is referring, and I don't think he is aware of it, to the pirates.

The mother, naturally, cries. How many times must she have cried without realizing it, while she made a meal, or the beds, or did the laundry. As though she were coughing or sneezing. Her children don't look at her. Her husband, on the other hand, moves a hand closer to her and she takes it as if he were passing her the salt or the bread, in any case something that she has asked for because she needs it.

When I am about to speak, to open the bag and give them the letter, the mother suddenly rises and disappears; we hear the sounds of drawers being opened and closed and after a while, she returns with a photograph album. She sits down with an awkward movement, moves her chair closer to mine, dragging it, opens the album, searches and finally finds the place where she wanted to be. She shows me a photo. She moves the glass of wine, which I haven't touched, to see it. Miguel says:

"That's Nelson, just before he went to Saint Helena."

I look, and what I see takes my breath away, because the person appearing in the photograph they are showing me is Dr. Prendel alone, young, smiling, with that charac-teristic expression of his, the expression that came over his mouth every time he was up to one of his old tricks.

I drink the entire glass of wine in one gulp. I look at the photograph again. The silence surrounding me is like the silence streaming through me.

I hear Miguel, still standing, ask me:

"And how did you know my brother?"

I think quickly. I remember what my grandfather used to say: "Little one, one lie always leads to another; it's better to tell the truth from the beginning." But now I am the one with a secret and I want to keep it to myself. Did I know Nelson Souza? I am aware that everyone is waiting for an answer. And the impulse comes on its own, and I give myself up to it as I bury the letter in the bottom of my bag. I say:

"I am the widow of the only man who came to really know him. It is a long story." And I realize I will have to invent it, rewrite his life while I speak.

The mother rises, says:

"You'll stay for lunch, of course." And she asks Lidia to put on the floral tablecloth and Miguel to go down and get nice wine and dessert. And turning to me she clarifies, "We used to have a grocery store but not now. We're retired."

It is clear that I cannot refuse. The family machinery has begun to function and it can't be stopped.

I leave that house when it is already dark. I told a lot of lies. Anyone, once their back is to the wall, can do it. I made up a story that consoled them. I told them that Nelson had saved Prendel and in saving him had died. It is, when you get right down to it, a truth told in a particular way.

I walk through the streets of the Alfama neighborhood, erect as the truth that has been revealed to me and that I have decided to keep for myself alone. I feel I have that right.

I find a wastebin, stop, take Nelson Souza's letter from my bag, tear it up, and throw it away. I don't know if it is an act of love or revenge.

Acknowledgements

To Esther Rovira, who never puts off till later what we need now.

To Eva Gutiérrez, "doctor of me," for her generosity.

To my sister, Marina Company, for her unconditional support.

To María Schjaer, for one more book.

To my editors, Silvia Querini and Josep Lluch, for the trust and common path we've started down together.

EUROPA EDITIONS BACKLIST
(alphabetical by author)

Fiction

Carmine Abate
Between Two Seas • 978-1-933372-40-2 • Territories: World
The Homecoming Party • 978-1-933372-83-9 • Territories:
World

Milena Agus
From the Land of the Moon • 978-1-60945-001-4 • Ebook •
Territories: World (excl. ANZ)

Salwa Al Neimi
The Proof of the Honey • 978-1-933372-68-6 • Ebook •
Territories: World (excl UK)

Simonetta Agnello Hornby
The Nun • 978-1-60945-062-5 • Territories: World

Daniel Arsand
Lovers • 978-1-60945-071-7 • Ebook • Territories: World

Jenn Ashworth
A Kind of Intimacy • 978-1-933372-86-0 • Territories: US & Can

Beryl Bainbridge
The Girl in the Polka Dot Dress • 978-1-60945-056-4 • Ebook •
Territories: US

Muriel Barbery
The Elegance of the Hedgehog • 978-1-933372-60-0 • Ebook •
Territories: World (excl. UK & EU)
Gourmet Rhapsody • 978-1-933372-95-2 • Ebook • Territories:
World (excl. UK & EU)

Stefano Benni
Margherita Dolce Vita • 978-1-933372-20-4 • Territories: World
Timeskipper • 978-1-933372-44-0 • Territories: World

Romano Bilenchi
The Chill • 978-1-933372-90-7 • Territories: World

Kazimierz Brandys
Rondo • 978-1-60945-004-5 • Territories: World

Alina Bronsky
Broken Glass Park • 978-1-933372-96-9 • Ebook • Territories:
World
The Hottest Dishes of the Tartar Cuisine • 978-1-60945-006-9 •
Ebook • Territories: World

Jesse Browner
Everything Happens Today • 978-1-60945-051-9 • Ebook •
Territories: World (excl. UK & EU)

Francisco Coloane
Tierra del Fuego • 978-1-933372-63-1 • Ebook • Territories:
World

Rebecca Connell
The Art of Losing • 978-1-933372-78-5 • Territories: US

Laurence Cossé
A Novel Bookstore • 978-1-933372-82-2 • Ebook • Territories:
World
An Accident in August • 978-1-60945-049-6 • Territories: World
(excl. UK)

Diego De Silva
I Hadn't Understood • 978-1-60945-065-6 • Territories: World

Shashi Deshpande
The Dark Holds No Terrors • 978-1-933372-67-9 • Territories: US

Steve Erickson
Zeroville • 978-1-933372-39-6 • Territories: US & Can
These Dreams of You • 978-1-60945-063-2 • Territories: US & Can

Elena Ferrante
The Days of Abandonment • 978-1-933372-00-6 • Ebook •
Territories: World
Troubling Love • 978-1-933372-16-7 • Territories: World
The Lost Daughter • 978-1-933372-42-6 • Territories: World

Linda Ferri
Cecilia • 978-1-933372-87-7 • Territories: World

Damon Galgut
In a Strange Room • 978-1-60945-011-3 • Ebook • Territories: USA

Santiago Gamboa
Necropolis • 978-1-60945-073-1 • Ebook • Territories: World

Jane Gardam
Old Filth • 978-1-933372-13-6 • Ebook • Territories: US
The Queen of the Tambourine • 978-1-933372-36-5 • Ebook •
Territories: US
The People on Privilege Hill • 978-1-933372-56-3 • Ebook •
Territories: US
The Man in the Wooden Hat • 978-1-933372-89-1 • Ebook •
Territories: US
God on the Rocks • 978-1-933372-76-1 • Ebook • Territories: US
Crusoe's Daughter • 978-1-60945-069-4 • Ebook • Territories: US

Anna Gavalda
French Leave • 978-1-60945-005-2 • Ebook • Territories: US & Can

Seth Greenland
The Angry Buddhist • 978-1-60945-068-7 • Ebook • Territories:
World

Katharina Hacker
The Have-Nots • 978-1-933372-41-9 • Territories: World
(excl. India)

Patrick Hamilton
Hangover Square • 978-1-933372-06-8 • Territories: US & Can

James Hamilton-Paterson
Cooking with Fernet Branca • 978-1-933372-01-3 • Territories: US
Amazing Disgrace • 978-1-933372-19-8 • Territories: US
Rancid Pansies • 978-1-933372-62-4 • Territories: USA

Alfred Hayes
The Girl on the Via Flaminia • 978-1-933372-24-2 • Ebook •
Territories: World

Jean-Claude Izzo
The Lost Sailors • 978-1-933372-35-8 • Territories: World
A Sun for the Dying • 978-1-933372-59-4 • Territories: World

Gail Jones
Sorry • 978-1-933372-55-6 • Territories: US & Can

Ioanna Karystiani
The Jasmine Isle • 978-1-933372-10-5 • Territories: World
Swell • 978-1-933372-98-3 • Territories: World

Peter Kocan
Fresh Fields • 978-1-933372-29-7 • Territories: US, EU & Can
The Treatment and the Cure • 978-1-933372-45-7 • Territories:
US, EU & Can

Helmut Krausser
Eros • 978-1-933372-58-7 • Territories: World

Amara Lakhous
Clash of Civilizations Over an Elevator in Piazza Vittorio •
978-1-933372-61-7 • Ebook • Territories: World
Divorce Islamic Style • 978-1-60945-066-3 • Ebook • Territories:
World

Lia Levi
The Jewish Husband • 978-1-933372-93-8 • Territories: World

Valerio Massimo Manfredi
The Ides of March • 978-1-933372-99-0 • Territories: US

Leïla Marouane
The Sexual Life of an Islamist in Paris • 978-1-933372-85-3 •
Territories: World

Lorenzo Mediano
The Frost on His Shoulders • 978-1-60945-072-4 • Ebook •
Territories: World

Sélim Nassib
I Loved You for Your Voice • 978-1-933372-07-5 • Territories:
World
The Palestinian Lover • 978-1-933372-23-5 • Territories: World

Amélie Nothomb
Tokyo Fiancée • 978-1-933372-64-8 • Territories: US & Can
Hygiene and the Assassin • 978-1-933372-77-8 • Ebook •
Territories: US & Can

Valeria Parrella
For Grace Received • 978-1-933372-94-5 • Territories: World

Alessandro Piperno
The Worst Intentions • 978-1-933372-33-4 • Territories: World
Persecution • 978-1-60945-074-8 • Ebook • Territories: World

Lorcan Roche
The Companion • 978-1-933372-84-6 • Territories: World

Boualem Sansal
The German Mujahid • 978-1-933372-92-1 • Ebook •
Territories: US & Can

Eric-Emmanuel Schmitt
The Most Beautiful Book in the World • 978-1-933372-74-7 •
Ebook • Territories: World
The Woman with the Bouquet • 978-1-933372-81-5 • Ebook •
Territories: US & Can

Angelika Schrobsdorff
You Are Not Like Other Mothers • 978-1-60945-075-5 • Ebook
• Territories: World

Audrey Schulman
Three Weeks in December • 978-1-60945-064-9 • Ebook •
Territories: US & Can

James Scudamore
Heliopolis • 978-1-933372-73-0 • Ebook • Territories: US

Luis Sepúlveda
The Shadow of What We Were • 978-1-60945-002-1 • Ebook •
Territories: World

Paolo Sorrentino
Everybody's Right • 978-1-60945-052-6 • Ebook • Territories:
US & Can

Domenico Starnone
First Execution • 978-1-933372-66-2 • Territories: World

Henry Sutton
Get Me out of Here • 978-1-60945-007-6 • Ebook • Territories:
US & Can

Chad Taylor
Departure Lounge • 978-1-933372-09-9 • Territories: US, EU &
Can

Roma Tearne
Mosquito • 978-1-933372-57-0 • Territories: US & Can
Bone China • 978-1-933372-75-4 • Territories: US

André Carl van der Merwe
Moffie • 978-1-60945-050-2 • Ebook • Territories: World
(excl. S. Africa)

Fay Weldon
Chalcot Crescent • 978-1-933372-79-2 • Territories: US

Anne Wiazemsky
My Berlin Child • 978-1-60945-003-8 • Territories: US & Can

Jonathan Yardley
Second Reading • 978-1-60945-008-3 • Ebook • Territories: US
& Can

Edwin M. Yoder Jr.
Lions at Lamb House • 978-1-933372-34-1 • Territories: World

Michele Zackheim
Broken Colors • 978-1-933372-37-2 • Territories: World

Alice Zeniter
Take This Man • 978-1-60945-053-3 • Territories: World

Tonga Books

Ian Holding
Of Beasts and Beings • 978-1-60945-054-0 • Ebook • Territories:
US & Can

Sara Levine
Treasure Island!!! • 978-0-14043-768-3 • Ebook • Territories: World

Alexander Maksik
You Deserve Nothing • 978-1-60945-048-9 • Ebook • Territories: US, Can & EU (excl. UK)

Thad Ziolkowski
Wichita • 978-1-60945-070-0 • Ebook • Territories: World

Crime/Noir

Massimo Carlotto
The Goodbye Kiss • 978-1-933372-05-1 • Ebook • Territories: World
Death's Dark Abyss • 978-1-933372-18-1 • Ebook • Territories: World
The Fugitive • 978-1-933372-25-9 • Ebook • Territories: World
Bandit Love • 978-1-933372-80-8 • Ebook • Territories: World
Poisonville • 978-1-933372-91-4 • Ebook • Territories: World

Giancarlo De Cataldo
The Father and the Foreigner • 978-1-933372-72-3 • Territories: World

Caryl Férey
Zulu • 978-1-933372-88-4 • Ebook • Territories: World
(excl. UK & EU)
Utu • 978-1-60945-055-7 • Ebook • Territories: World
(excl. UK & EU)

Alicia Giménez-Bartlett
Dog Day • 978-1-933372-14-3 • Territories: US & Can
Prime Time Suspect • 978-1-933372-31-0 • Territories: US & Can
Death Rites • 978-1-933372-54-9 • Territories: US & Can

Jean-Claude Izzo
Total Chaos • 978-1-933372-04-4 • Territories: US & Can
Chourmo • 978-1-933372-17-4 • Territories: US & Can
Solea • 978-1-933372-30-3 • Territories: US & Can

Matthew F. Jones
Boot Tracks • 978-1-933372-11-2 • Territories: US & Can

Gene Kerrigan
The Midnight Choir • 978-1-933372-26-6 • Territories: US & Can
Little Criminals • 978-1-933372-43-3 • Territories: US & Can

Carlo Lucarelli
Carte Blanche • 978-1-933372-15-0 • Territories: World
The Damned Season • 978-1-933372-27-3 • Territories: World
Via delle Oche • 978-1-933372-53-2 • Territories: World

Edna Mazya
Love Burns • 978-1-933372-08-2 • Territories: World (excl. ANZ)

Yishai Sarid
Limassol • 978-1-60945-000-7 • Ebook • Territories: World
(excl. UK, AUS & India)

Joel Stone
The Jerusalem File • 978-1-933372-65-5 • Ebook • Territories:
World

Benjamin Tammuz
Minotaur • 978-1-933372-02-0 • Ebook • Territories: World

Non-fiction

Alberto Angela
A Day in the Life of Ancient Rome • 978-1-933372-71-6 •
Territories: World • History

Helmut Dubiel
Deep In the Brain: Living with Parkinson's Disease •
978-1-933372-70-9 • Ebook • Territories: World •
Medicine/Memoir

James Hamilton-Paterson
Seven-Tenths: The Sea and Its Thresholds • 978-1-933372-69-3 •
Territories: USA • Nature/Essays

www.europaeditions.com

Daniele Mastrogiacomo
Days of Fear • 978-1-933372-97-6 • Ebook • Territories: World
• Current affairs/Memoir/Afghanistan/Journalism

Valery Panyushkin
Twelve Who Don't Agree • 978-1-60945-010-6 • Ebook •
Territories: World • Current affairs/Memoir/Russia/Journalism

Christa Wolf
One Day a Year: 1960-2000 • 978-1-933372-22-8 • Territories:
World • Memoir/History/20th Century

Children's Illustrated Fiction

Altan
Here Comes Timpa • 978-1-933372-28-0 • Territories: World
(excl. Italy)
Timpa Goes to the Sea • 978-1-933372-32-7 • Territories: World
(excl. Italy)
Fairy Tale Timpa • 978-1-933372-38-9 • Territories: World
(excl. Italy)

Wolf Erlbruch
The Big Question • 978-1-933372-03-7 • Territories: US & Can
The Miracle of the Bears • 978-1-933372-21-1 • Territories: US
& Can
(with **Gioconda Belli**) *The Butterfly Workshop* •
978-1-933372-12-9 • Territories: US & Can